MW00772197

BA

THE MILLINER'S HAT MYSTERY

SIR BASIL HOME THOMSON (1861-1939) was educated at Eton and New College Oxford. After spending a year farming in Iowa, he married in 1889 and worked for the Foreign Service. This included a stint working alongside the Prime Minister of Tonga (according to some accounts, he *was* the Prime Minister of Tonga) in the 1890s followed by a return to the Civil Service and a period as Governor of Dartmoor Prison. He was Assistant Commissioner to the Metropolitan Police from 1913 to 1919, after which he moved into Intelligence. He was knighted in 1919 and received other honours from Europe and Japan, but his public career came to an end when he was arrested for committing an act of indecency in Hyde Park in 1925 – an incident much debated and disputed.

His eight crime novels featuring series character Inspector Richardson were written in the 1930's and received great praise from Dorothy L. Sayers among others. He also wrote biographical and criminological works.

Also by Basil Thomson

BASIL THOMSON

THE MILLINER'S HAT MYSTERY

With an introduction by
Martin Edwards

DEAN STREET PRESS

Published by Dean Street Press 2016

All Rights Reserved

First published in 1937 by Eldon Press

Cover by DSP

Introduction © Martin Edwards 2016

ISBN 978 1 911095 79 8

www.deanstreetpress.co.uk

To my sister

ZOE HOYLE

In hope that she will forgive the use
to which I have put her imposing
row of barns

Introduction

SIR BASIL THOMSON's stranger-than-fiction life was packed so full of incident that one can understand why his work as a crime novelist has been rather overlooked. This was a man whose CV included spells as a colonial administrator, prison governor, intelligence officer, and Assistant Commissioner at Scotland Yard. Among much else, he worked alongside the Prime Minister of Tonga (according to some accounts, he *was* the Prime Minister of Tonga), interrogated Mata Hari and Roger Casement (although not at the same time), and was sensationally convicted of an offence of indecency committed in Hyde Park. More than three-quarters of a century after his death, he deserves to be recognised for the contribution he made to developing the police procedural, a form of detective fiction that has enjoyed lasting popularity.

Basil Home Thomson was born in 1861 – the following year his father became Archbishop of York – and was educated at Eton before going up to New College. He left Oxford after a couple of terms, apparently as a result of suffering depression, and joined the Colonial Service. Assigned to Fiji, he became a stipendiary magistrate before moving to Tonga. Returning to England in 1893, he published *South Sea Yarns*, which is among the 22 books written by him which are listed in Allen J. Hubin's comprehensive bibliography of crime fiction (although in some cases, the criminous content was limited).

Thomson was called to the Bar, but opted to become deputy governor of Liverpool Prison; he later served as governor of such prisons as Dartmoor and Wormwood Scrubs, and acted as secretary to the Prison Commission. In 1913, he became head of C.I.D., which acted as the enforcement arm of British military intelligence after war broke out. When the

Dutch exotic dancer and alleged spy Mata Hari arrived in England in 1916, she was arrested and interviewed at length by Thomson at Scotland Yard; she was released, only to be shot the following year by a French firing squad. He gave an account of the interrogation in *Queer People* (1922).

Thomson was knighted, and given the additional responsibility of acting as Director of Intelligence at the Home Office, but in 1921, he was controversially ousted, prompting a heated debate in Parliament: according to *The Times*, "for a few minutes there was pandemonium". The government argued that Thomson was at odds with the Commissioner of the Metropolitan Police, Sir William Horwood (whose own career ended with an ignominious departure fromoffice seven years later), but it seems likely be that covert political machinations lay behind his removal. With many aspects of Thomson's complex life, it is hard to disentangle fiction from fact.

Undaunted, Thomson resumed his writing career, and in 1925, he published *Mr Pepper Investigates*, a collection of humorous short mysteries, the most renowned of which is "The Vanishing of Mrs Fraser". In the same year, he was arrested in Hyde Park for "committing an act in violation of public decency" with a young woman who gave her name as Thelma de Lava. Thomson protested his innocence, but in vain: his trial took place amid a blaze of publicity, and he was fined five pounds. Despite the fact that Thelma de Lava had pleaded guilty (her fine was reportedly paid by a photographer), Thomson launched an appeal, claiming that he was the victim of a conspiracy, but the court would have none of it. Was he framed, or the victim of entrapment? If so, was the reason connected with his past work in intelligence or crime solving? The answers remain uncertain, but Thomson's equivocal responses to the police after being apprehended damaged his credibility.

Public humiliation of this kind would have broken a less formidable man, but Thomson, by now in his mid-sixties, proved astonishingly resilient. A couple of years after his trial, he was appointed to reorganise the Siamese police force, and he continued to produce novels. These included *The Kidnapper* (1933), which Dorothy L. Sayers described in a review for the *Sunday Times* as "not so much a detective story as a sprightly fantasia upon a detective theme." She approved the fact that Thomson wrote "good English very amusingly", and noted that "some of his characters have real charm." Mr Pepper returned in *The Kidnapper*, but in the same year, Thomson introduced his most important character, a Scottish policeman called Richardson.

Thomson took advantage of his inside knowledge to portray a young detective climbing through the ranks at Scotland Yard. And Richardson's rise is amazingly rapid: thanks to the fastest fast-tracking imaginable, he starts out as a police constable, and has become Chief Constable by the time of his seventh appearance – in a book published only four years after the first. We learn little about Richardson's background beyond the fact that he comes of Scottish farming stock, but he is likeable as well as highly efficient, and his sixth case introduces him to his future wife. His inquiries take him – and other colleagues – not only to different parts of England but also across the Channel on more than one occasion: in *The Case of the Dead Diplomat*, all the action takes place in France. There is a zest about the stories, especially when compared with some of the crime novels being produced at around the same time, which is striking, especially given that all of them were written by a man in his seventies.

From the start of the series, Thomson takes care to show the team work necessitated by a criminal investigation. Richardson is a key connecting figure, but the importance of his colleagues' efforts is never minimised in order to highlight his brilliance. In *The Case of the Dead Diplomat*, for instance, it is the trusty Sergeant Cooper who makes good use of his linguistic skills and flair for impersonation to trap the villains of the piece. Inspector Vincent takes centre stage in *The Milliner's Hat Mystery*, with Richardson confined to the background. He is more prominent in *A Murder is Arranged*, but it is Inspector Dallas who does most of the leg-work.

Such a focus on police team-working is very familiar to present day crime fiction fans, but it was something fresh in the Thirties. Yet Thomson was not the first man with personal experience of police life to write crime fiction: Frank Froest, a legendary detective, made a considerable splash with his first novel, *The Grell Mystery*, published in 1913. Froest, though, was a career cop, schooled in "the university of life" without the benefit of higher education, who sought literary input from a journalist, George Dilnot, whereas Basil Thomson was a fluent and experienced writer whose light, brisk style is ideally suited to detective fiction, with its emphasis on entertainment. Like so many other detective novelists, his interest in "true crime" is occasionally apparent in his fiction, but although *Who Killed Stella Pomeroy?* opens with a murder scenario faintly reminiscent of the legendary Wallace case of 1930, the storyline soon veers off in a quite different direction.

Even before Richardson arrived on the scene, two accomplished detective novelists had created successful police series. Freeman Wills Crofts devised elaborate crimes (often involving ingenious alibis) for Inspector French to solve, and his books highlight the patience and meticulous work of the skilled police investigator. Henry Wade wrote increasingly ambitious novels, often featuring the Oxford-educated Inspector Poole, and exploring the tensions between police colleagues as well as their shared values. Thomson's mysteries are less convoluted than Crofts', and less sophisticated than Wade's, but they make pleasant reading. This is, at least in part, thanks to little touches of detail that are unquestionably authentic – such as senior officers' dread of newspaper criticism, as in *The Dartmoor Enigma*. No other crime writer, after all, has ever had such wide-ranging personal experience of prison management, intelligence work, the hierarchies of Scotland Yard, let alone a desperate personal fight, under the unforgiving glare of the media spotlight, to prove his innocence of a criminal charge sure to stain, if not destroy, his reputation.

Ingenuity was the hallmark of many of the finest detective novels written during "the Golden Age of murder" between the wars, and intricacy of plotting – at least judged by the standards of Agatha Christie, Anthony Berkeley, and John Dickson Carr – was not Thomson's true speciality. That said, *The Milliner's Hat Mystery* is remarkable for having inspired Ian Fleming, while he was working in intelligence during the Second World War, after Thomson's death. In a memo to Rear Admiral John Godfrey, Fleming said: "The following suggestion is used in a book by Basil Thomson: a corpse dressed as an airman, with despatches in his pockets, could be dropped on the coast, supposedly from a parachute that has failed. I understand there is no difficulty in obtaining corpses at the Naval Hospital, but, of course, it would have to be a fresh one." This clever idea became the basis for "Operation Mincemeat", a plan to conceal the invasion of Italy from North Africa.

A further intriguing connection between Thomson and Fleming is that Thomson inscribed copies of at least two of the Richardson books to Kathleen Pettigrew, who was personal assistant to the Director of MI6, Stewart Menzies. She is widely regarded as the woman on whom Fleming based Miss Moneypenny, secretary to James Bond's boss M – the Moneypenny character was originally called "Petty" Petteval. Possibly it was through her that Fleming came across Thomson's book.

Thomson's writing was of sufficiently high calibre to prompt Dorothy L. Sayers to heap praise on Richardson's performance in his third case: "he puts in some of that excellent, sober, straightforward detective work which he so well knows how to do and follows the clue of a post-mark to the heart of a very plausible and proper mystery. I find him a most agreeable companion." The acerbic American critics Jacques Barzun and Wendell Hertig Taylor also had a soft spot for Richardson, saying in *A Catalogue of Crime* that his investigations amount to "early police routine minus the contrived bickering, stomach ulcers, and pub-crawling with which later writers have masked poverty of invention and the dullness of repetitive questioning".

Books in the Richardson series have been out of print and hard to find for decades, and their reappearance at affordable prices is as welcome as it is overdue. Now that Dean Street Press have republished all eight recorded entries in the Richardson case-book, twenty-first century readers are likely to find his company just as agreeable as Sayers did.

Martin Edwards
www.martinedwardsbooks.com

Chapter One

THE CORONER'S COURT at Oldbury was crowded, for the news had spread that the inquest about to be held was concerned with a death that was likely to prove more mysterious than any that the police had had to deal with within the memory of man. The coroner took his seat at his table and the hum of conversation was hushed. He called Leslie Griffith. A young man stood up and came forward.

"You are a clerk in the Local Government Board in London?"

"I am."

"And on July 31st you drove your car into a barn for shelter from a violent thunderstorm."

"Yes."

"Were you alone in the car?"

"No, my friend Douglas Powell was with me."

"What did you find in that barn?"

"We found the body of a man."

"How was it lying?"

"Parallel with the left wall. I stumbled over it in getting out; in fact I fell over it. Owing to the thunderstorm it was as dark as night."

"What did you do?"

"I picked myself up and called to my friend, and we went over together to the house opposite and explained to the owner what had happened and asked leave to use the telephone."

"Did you telephone to the police?"

"No; Mr Howard, the owner of the house, telephoned to Dr Travers. He was afraid that in entering the barn we had knocked over his deaf gardener."

"While you were waiting for the doctor did anyone touch the body?"

"We waited in the house until the doctor arrived and then we went back to the barn with him; we found the body lying just as we had left it."

The coroner called Douglas Powell.

"Do you corroborate the evidence of the last witness?"

"Yes sir."

"Were you at the wheel of your car?"

"I was."

"Are you quite sure that you did not collide with the deceased and knock him down?"

"Quite sure. I was going at a foot's pace and I should have felt the shock."

Dr Henry Travers was the next witness.

"You were called by telephone to the barn in the grounds of Hatch Court? What did you find?"

"The dead body of a man aged between forty and fifty; I examined the body and found a bullet wound in the head. The body was cooling; death had occurred from three to four hours before I saw it."

"Did you telephone to the police?"

"I did, and Inspector Miller came from Oldbury."

"John Miller," called the coroner, and a man in the uniform of a police inspector stood up.

"You were called by telephone to see a man who had been found shot through the head?"

"I was."

"You concluded that he had been murdered?"

"Yes, because I found neither pistol nor rifle in the barn, nor any bullet hole in the walls or roof."

"How do you account for the body being there?"

"It must have been brought there in a vehicle, most probably a car. The shoes were clean as if they had only just been put on."

"Was a car seen by anyone?"

"Yes, by Peter Bury, the deaf gardener. He was sheltering from the storm in a tool shed and thought he saw a big car enter the barn. It was not until the storm was over that he found the little car belonging to Mr Powell in the barn and thought that the big one must have been a hallucination due to the lightning."

"Has the body been identified?"

"Not yet, sir. I searched the pockets very carefully and made an inventory of everything I found in them. Besides the objects carried by smokers I found the sum of £10 16s. 9d. in notes and silver."

"Did you notice anything of special importance in the things you found in the pockets?"

"Only that everything appeared to be brand new; even the notecase showed no sign of wear."

"Were there no visiting cards?"

"Yes sir, quite a number with name and address complete and the telephone number in the corner."

"Did that enable you to communicate with the deceased's friends?"

"No sir. I telephoned to the address given on the cards, but the operator informed me that there was no such number and no such address."

"Did you find any other document likely to help in iden-tification?"

"Yes sir, a passport in the same name—John Whitaker."

"The passport is being verified?"

"Yes sir, we are taking every possible step to have the body identified. My chief constable has been in telephonic communication with Scotland Yard and has asked for help. No doubt a senior officer will be detailed from the Yard to take charge of the enquiries."

"In that case, gentlemen of the jury, I shall have no option but to adjourn the inquest until the police have had time to complete their enquiries. The inquest is adjourned. You will be notified in due course by my officer when it will be reopened."

Inspector Miller spent a few minutes in going round among the witnesses and saying a word or two to each. As he was leaving the building a tall, good-looking man, who had been waiting by the door, stood up and addressed him.

"I must introduce myself, Mr Miller—Chief Inspector Vincent from the Yard. I was told to lose no time in coming down here and I was fortunate enough to arrive in time to hear a good part of the evidence given at the inquest."

"I'm very glad you've come, Mr Vincent. You see the difficulty that I am up against. This man was shot either in some other locality or in a car— 'taken for a ride,' in fact, as they say in America."

"Do you think that the man was deliberately trying to hide his identity, or that his assailants were doing that for him and for themselves?"

"So far there has been nothing to give the answer to that question. Until we know his identity it is useless to speculate about the motive for the murder."

"May I ask what steps you have already taken for establishing his identity?"

"The usual steps—searching the list of missing persons in the police publications. I have a mass of papers at the office, which of course are at your service. My car is here." He made a signal to the uniformed driver of his car and, though the distance to police headquarters was barely half a mile, they jumped in.

"I brought a sergeant down with me," said Vincent. "We shall find him at your office."

"Is he the man who usually works with you?"

"Yes. Detective-Sergeant Walker."

"Then I feel sure that he is a live wire."

Miller had been taking stock of his companion and had decided that he belonged to a type of detective that was new to him. To begin with, his accent was not that of the ordinary police officer. It was what, for want of a better adjective, was described as an educated accent. Miller was curious to know what had brought a man of university education into the police, but of course he could not put so personal a question to an officer of this rank. He did go so far as to ask him whether he knew Superintendent Richardson. Vincent at once rose to the bait.

"You have deprived him of a step in rank. He is now my chief constable, and he is one of the few promoted from the ranks whose promotion has given lively satisfaction throughout the whole service. I, myself, am proud to be working under him."

They had reached the police station. Inspector Miller invited Vincent into his room where they found Sergeant Walker awaiting them.

"There, Chief Inspector, that pile of papers is for you to look through. You will find reports from a number of my officers about missing persons, but so far they have produced nothing."

"When was the body found?"

"Only the day before yesterday—Saturday. You will see that we have wasted no time."

"The persons I should like to see first are those two young men who found the body. Where are they to be found?"

Miller looked a little crestfallen. "The fact is, Chief Inspector, that I allowed them to continue their journey to Cornwall, after taking their addresses, of course. They promised to return on receipt of a telegram if they were wanted. You will find their statements on the top of those papers and I don't think that they are able to give any further information. That is why I let them go."

"Have you found any further trace of the big car which the deaf gardener thought he had seen during the thunderstorm?"

"No. He appears to have been the only man in the village who saw it and I doubt whether his evidence can be relied upon. You know the type of witness who comes forward with a story, and then when he finds that the police attach importance to it he embroiders it with all kinds of detail drawn from his imagination."

"I know the type, but I think that he must be the first witness that I interview. The question is whether I should see him here or, less formally, on his own ground at Hatch Court. I think that Hatch Court would be best because I could make an inspection of the barn at the same time."

"It'll take us no time at all to get to Hatch Court if you will jump into the car again, Mr Vincent. Would you like your sergeant to come with us?"

"Yes, because he's accustomed to taking down notes as we go. What has the owner of Hatch Court to say to the irruption of police on to his premises?"

"Mr Howard? Oh, he's given us a free hand. We needn't even trouble to ask for him. As long as he knows in due course what conclusion we come to, he'll ask no questions."

"So much the better. The only member of the staff we want to see is that deaf gardener and we can see him in the barn itself."

They had no difficulty in finding Peter Bury— indeed, since the thunderstorm and his supposed hallucination he seemed to have been doing little more than watch the barn from some secret hiding place for some other strange occurrence. Miller beckoned to him to approach. He shambled towards the two police officers with a hesitating gait.

Vincent called him into the barn and, using his two hands as a megaphone, shouted: "I want you to take us to where you were standing when you saw that car outside the barn." He had to repeat the question in a louder tone before intelligence dawned in the old man's face. He touched Vincent on the arm, making a gesture towards the garden. Vincent followed him.

Arrived outside a little tool shed, the old gardener conducted his part of the conversation in dumb show, intimating that they were standing on the very spot from which he saw the car swing round into the barnyard. Then he found his voice.

"An old friend of mine once got struck by lightning and had to go all doubled up for the rest of his life. I've been shy of lightning ever since. That's why I was sheltering."

Vincent's voice rang out: "Did—you—see—the car—go—into—the barn?"

"I saw it swing round from the lane into the yard and I said to meself: 'You'll never get a car as big as that into the barn, if that's what you're after.' And then the lightning flashed again and I took cover."

"And when you came out from your cover you found a little car in the barn."

"That's right, though how I could have made such a mistake beats me—taking a little car for a big one."

"Thank you, Peter. If we want you again we'll come and find you." Turning to Miller, Vincent said: "Now let us go to the barn."

The floor of the barn was covered deep in dust. It showed clearly the wheel marks of a small car, and Miller pointed out a shallow depression in the dust which he said had been made by the dead body and a medley of footprints all round it.

"As you see, there are no marks here of any big car having entered. These wheel marks were made by the car belonging to those two young men."

"Yes, and of course the footprints explain themselves. Now, assuming that Peter Bury did see a big car stop outside the barn, let us reconstruct the scene. The car drew up here, but in that heavy storm all wheel marks would naturally be washed away. Peter Bury would not have seen what happened when the car stopped, but obviously two men must have been required to carry the dead body into the barn; their proceedings were masked by the car. Then what happened? The men returned to their seats, the car swung round in this direction in the act of turning to leave the yard. It was rather a sharp turn for a big car to get round without manoeuvring." Vincent appeared to be talking to himself rather than to his companion, whom he left and walked rapidly over to the low wall of the yard. Miller could not help admiring the quickness and agility of his movements. It was as if he was on wires. He stopped at the low wall and stooped. "Yes, here we are," he said over his shoulder; "it was too sharp a turn for a big car. Look at this streak of black. That is car varnish from one of the wings. The driver was in a hurry—he didn't stop to back—stripped the wing clean of varnish and, no doubt, made a biggish dent in it. That will be something to go by in hunting for the car."

"None of the servants saw a big car," objected Miller, "and, as you see, their windows look out this way."

"They do, but have you ever seen a house full of maids in a thunderstorm? They run to cover, preferably under a bed or in a linen closet. The storm was a stroke of luck for our murderers."

Vincent was silent as they walked back to Miller's car. When they had taken their seats he asked: "Have you made any enquiries at garages down the Bath Road about a car with a dinted offside wing? Garage hands notice these things."

"Not yet," replied Miller half apologetically. "We had so little to go upon."

Vincent relapsed into another silence and then he said: "If the man was shot in the car there must be a bullet mark somewhere at the level of a man's head. That theory might be worth pursuing."

Miller was spared from answering this remark by the sight of a small car drawn up before the police headquarters.

"Hallo!" he said. "What's this?"

He was not long left in doubt. A young man, whom Vincent recognized as having been one of the witnesses at the inquest, jumped out of the car and made a sign to Miller to pull up.

"We have something that will interest you, Inspector, and we brought it back from a garage a few miles down the road for you to see."

"What is it?"

"A car window with what looks like a bullet hole clean through it."

Chapter Two

THE THREE police officers jumped out of their car.

"Where is this window?" asked Miller.

"We took it into the police station and left it with your station sergeant."

Miller hurried into the building, followed by the others. Griffith constituted himself showman. The window was standing propped again the wall.

"Now you can see what a car window looks like when it's had a bullet through it."

"Yes," said Vincent; "there's been dirty work at the crossroads. Do you see what started the fracture—that round hole with little cracks radiating from it in every direction. This is no ordinary break: that window was broken by a pistol shot. Where did you find it?"

"At a garage about four miles down the Bath Road. Here is their card. They told us that the window came out of a sixteen-horse Daimler. Here's its number. It was quite by chance that we went into the garage at all; one of our plugs was missing fire badly and it was a case of any port in a storm. While they were changing the plug, Powell began poking about and saw this window propped up against the wall. He spotted at once that it was no ordinary break and after a little difficulty we got the garage people to let us have it for a bob."

"Did they give you a description of the driver?" asked Vincent.

"No, because we thought that if we started questioning they might take us for detectives and shut up like oysters. We did find out that the car came in on Saturday. I would offer you a seat in our little bus if there was room and run you down to the garage."

"Thank you very much, but I weigh over twelve stone and I should prove to be the last straw for your little car. Happily Inspector Miller has a car, and if you will wait until I've sent my sergeant back to London with this broken window we can start whenever you like."

"If you like to give me a seat in Inspector Miller's car I can act as your guide to the garage and let my friend follow us. It 'll save time."

"It's very kind of you," said Vincent; "I'll be ready in three minutes."

He was as good as his word; in three minutes he was at the wheel and had started up the engine. As soon as they were clear of the traffic, Griffith began to talk: he was prone to conversation.

"You'll excuse my curiosity, but I don't think you can belong to the county constabulary."

"No, I come from further afield."

"I felt sure you did: you must be from Scotland Yard. They've sent you down to take charge of the case. You must be one of the big four."

"You mean the big four of newspaper notoriety? I'm Chief Inspector Vincent."

"You're starting in this case with practically no clue at all, I gathered from the evidence at the inquest —not even the man's identity."

"That is so."

"I've often envied you your job when I read of criminal cases in the papers; it must be an exciting kind of life."

Vincent smiled. "It's all right when there are exciting episodes, but much of the work is the dreary business of elimination."

"Elimination?"

"Yes, because we suffer from too much rather than too little help from the public. In any sensational crime letters pour in from well-meaning people, not only in this country but abroad, and one cannot afford to neglect any of them for fear that there may be a grain of wheat among the chaff. The discouraging part of the job lies in the sifting of this mass of information."

"It must require a lot of patience."

"Yes, it does. Sometimes one gets so discouraged that it is all one can do to carry on."

"The garage is only about a couple of hundred yards from here. I suppose you'd like to conduct your enquiry alone?"

"Not at all, but you will want to stop your friend when he arrives and you might look after my car while waiting for him."

Griffith assented with a sigh and watched the lithe figure enter the garage.

Vincent asked for the foreman, who was found in a pit under a car, busily engaged in examining the pinions in the gear box.

"You're wanted, Harry," a mechanic called down to him.

"Who wants me?"

"The police." And then in a hoarse whisper the youth added: "It's a blooming 'tec from Scotland Yard, so he says."

The foreman, a youth little older than his own mechanics, crawled out of his lair and faced Vincent, wiping a smear of oil from his countenance with a swab of cotton waste.

"I'm sorry to interrupt you in your work, foreman, but I want some information about that car that came in with a broken window two days ago. How many men were there in the car?"

"Two, I think it was. It was two, wasn't it, Charlie?"

"Yes; there was the fellow with his arm in a sling and the other bloke that kept looking at his watch."

"Did they say where they were going?"

"Oh, they made no secret about that. They said that they were going to Cornwall."

As the foreman turned back to his work the young mechanic became confidential. "If you are wanting information about those two men I can tell you something. When I was tuning up their car and they didn't know I could hear them I heard them talking about a motorboat that they were to catch at Newquay. I could see that the feller that kept looking at his watch was in a great stew about being late. 'God knows,' he said, 'what we'll do if he's gone off without us,' and the other one said: 'He's swine enough to do anything.' Then one of them caught sight of me and nudged the other, and they dried up."

Having gleaned all possible information from the garage, Vincent returned to his car. He found that Griffith's companion had arrived in his tiny overloaded conveyance and the two young men were talking.

"Ah, here comes the chief inspector," said Griffith. "Now we shall be free to go on."

"Your discovery is going to prove very useful to me," said Vincent. "I found out that those two men were bound for Newquay to meet a motorboat and I must go on there, although they've had two days' start of me."

"We are bound for the west coast, too: we are going to Bude, which is not so very far away from Newquay, but you will travel much faster than we do and I suppose we must say good-bye."

"I'm afraid so. You will understand that I've no time to lose. Thank you once more for your help."

He started up the engine and slid away. As soon as he had cleared the built-up area and could let his car out, he began to think of what lay before him. He had the number of the car, that was something. He had Newquay as its destination; it might prove to be a difficult case if motorboats took part in it, but Vincent was not the man to welcome easy cases; the more difficult a case was, the better he liked it.

His first concern on arriving at Newquay was to make a round of the hotel garages in search of the car which had changed its broken window. He tried every hotel garage without success and then visited those which advertised the fact that they carried out repairs. In one of these, inconveniently situated in a narrow side street, he found what he was looking for—a sixteen-horse Daimler, with the number given by the garage in the Bath Road. It had a deep dint and scrape on the offside wing, exposing the metal. Vincent called the foreman.

"Who left this car here?" he asked.

The man was inclined to be jocular. "That would be telling," he said. "You've heard of the proverb: 'Ask no questions and they'll tell you no lies.'"

"Come," said Vincent, "I can't waste time bandying proverbs. I'm here to ask questions and you're here to answer them truthfully." He produced his official card and the young foreman stiffened with apprehension. "Now, perhaps you'll answer. Who left this car here?"

"Two gents who said they were leaving on a sea trip and would call for it when they came back. Is there anything wrong about them?"

"You can ask that question again when I've looked over the car."

The man stood back while Vincent made an examination of the seats and cushions of the interior. He was using a small square of damp blotting paper to soak up what he thought might be bloodstains, when the foreman, who was watching him keenly, interposed with a question:

"What are you looking for, sir?" he said.

"For bloodstains."

"Funny you should say that. The gent who left the car was fussing about the same thing. Very fussy he was, using a sponge and cotton waste to get it all off. He said there was nothing that damaged the fabric of the leather more than blood if it was allowed to dry on. It was his own blood, he said, from his elbow when he banged it through the window. It must have been a mighty bang to break triplex glass. He said that that was why he had his arm in a sling."

"Which arm was it?"

"Lord! To tell you the truth I couldn't say which. I remember thinking that it was funny that he should break one of the windows at the back of the car if he was at the wheel, as he was when he brought her in. He said that he had to drive in spite of his injured arm because the other chap couldn't."

"What did they look like?" asked Vincent.

"Oh, one was a big, heavy man, between thirty and forty, and the other a tall thin chap, a bit older."

"Well, I want you to put this car aside and not let anyone touch her—not even the owner if he turns up again—without letting me know. I shall be at the Raven Hotel and I'll come down at once if you ring up. You can't lock it up because, I suppose, the owner has the key, but you can stop any of your mechanics from interfering with it."

"Very good, sir; you can trust me to see that your orders are carried out."

While speaking Vincent had been trying to open the box at the rear of the car, which was locked.

"Do you want to get that open, sir?"

"Yes, but I suppose the owner has that key also."

"I daresay that I could manage to open it."

"What?" asked Vincent. "Have you fellows got duplicate keys for the boxes of every kind of car?"

The foreman laughed. "No sir, it's not as bad as that; but I served my apprenticeship with one of the firms that supply car manufacturers with these boxes and I've still got the tools for making both locks and keys. You needn't worry about my doing any damage: I'll open it all right and lock it up again."

"Very good, foreman; I'll be back again in about half an hour."

Vincent now decided to make enquiries at the quay. There he found the usual knot of fishermen and loafers in nautical costume. One of them, a bright-eyed man of about forty, constituted himself the mouthpiece of the party. Vincent knew the type—a type to beware of when one wants an exact register of facts, but quite useful where drama of the film complexion is sought. At first he avoided him and accosted a saturnine-looking ex-sailor who was smoking a foul clay pipe. He did not appear to be a man of many words, but that mattered little, for the others drifted up, the loquacious sailor with them.

"I hear you had a motor launch in here on Saturday and it picked up two men and went away with them."

The mariner nodded sourly without removing his pipe from the corner of his mouth, but the chatterbox, who was now within hearing, hastened to fill the breach.

"I saw those two gents; one of them had his arm in a sling. They kept asking us whether we'd seen their motorboat come in and go out again. I told them that it had been in, hanging about the best part of the day, and had then gone out again. That's right, isn't it, mates?" The rest nodded their assent. "I can tell you that the two gents were in a fine taking when they heard that she'd been in and gone out again—friends of the skipper, I suppose they were."

"But did she come in again?" asked Vincent.

"Yes, she did, and a bloke was standing up, sweeping the quay with his glasses. When he made out the two gents waving to him he brought the launch up to the steps, keeping the engine running. He hardly waited for them to step aboard, but pushed off and went full speed ahead."

"Do you know which way they went when they'd cleared the harbour?"

"No, one can't see that from here, but when the two gents were stepping aboard I heard the skipper say: 'Hurry up, Rupert, there's a southerly gale springing up, and if you're not nippy you'll be seasick like you were last time.' So I suppose she was bound for somewhere lying southwest of us."

"What kind of a boat was she?"

"Oh, she was a smart-looking craft, as fresh as paint could make her and big enough for any kind of sea."

"How many hands had she?"

"I only saw a boy besides the skipper, but the cabin looked as if there was accommodation for six at least."

"H'm! Quite a big boat," said Vincent, musing. "Anyway she could cross the Channel all right. Had she a name painted on her?"

"No, now I come to think of it she'd no name at all. That's funny. A craft like that generally has some fancy kind of name like Sunbeam painted all over her, but this one had nothing at all."

The taciturn smoker removed his pipe from his mouth, spat into the sea and spoke for the first time. "Shouldn't be surprised if there was something crooked about that boat—smuggling or something like that. The boy was a Frenchy—I heard him talking the lingo that those onion boys talk."

"And the skipper? Did he talk French, too?"

"When he spoke to the boy he did, but not when he took those two coves on board: then he spoke English all right, but it sounded funny."

"Thank you," said Vincent. "I think that must be the boat I wanted; I'm sorry they left before I got here."

Having finished his enquiries at the quay, Vincent returned to the garage. He found that the foreman had been as good as his word. He was obviously pleased with himself at having been able to exhibit his skill to a senior officer from the Yard.

"It was a job I can tell you, sir. I had to wait until the mechanics had knocked off work and gone home before I started on the key, but I managed it all right." He slid back the catches and raised the lid of the box. "There you are, sir, nothing in it but an old overcoat."

"Let me have a look at the coat."

It was a stout cold-resisting overcoat, evidently made by a good tailor. Vincent went rapidly through the pockets, but found nothing in them but crumbs of tobacco. He breathed more easily when he found an outfitter's label sewn under the tab of the collar.

"I'm going to take this car away with me, foreman, because it will be required as evidence in a murder case."

"But suppose the owner comes back and asks for it, what am I to tell him?"

"I don't think he will come back, but if he does you must ring up the Newquay police. I'm going on to leave the car with them."

"Very good, sir. You'll find her in good running order. The young lady at the desk will tell you what there is to pay."

Vincent made for the window where the lady sat enthroned behind her spectacles, with a ledger before her. The bill was quite moderate, but when Vincent made known his intention to carry off the car, she demurred.

"You see," she explained, "I gave the gentleman who left her here a receipt and if he comes back and finds his car gone, well..."

"You think he might make himself unpleasant."

"I won't say that. He seemed a nice well-mannered gentleman, but he might threaten an action at law, if you know what I mean."

"You mean that if you let her go out after giving a receipt for her, you might lose your situation?"

"Well, Mr Lutyens is a funny sort of gentleman: he might think that I was right, but he's just as likely to find fault and tell me that I ought to have rung him up before I let the car go. If you'll stop a minute I'll get on to him."

Vincent stopped a minute; the minute multiplied itself by five before the operator assured the speaker that there was no answer to her call. Hearing this Vincent declared his intention of driving the car to the police station and invited the lady to ring up the Newquay police to prepare them. On this she removed her ban and the car was driven out.

In consequence of this telephone message Vincent found the station sergeant waiting for him on the steps of the police station. To him Vincent explained the position. An inspector was called out and the car was formally handed over to be kept by the police until the chief constable received a communication from New Scotland Yard.

"Have you no clue at all to the identity of the murdered man?" asked the inspector.

"Five minutes ago I should have answered your question in the negative, but I have now one clue— a London tailor's name in the collar of an overcoat —Mendel in Sackville

Street. Luckily the manager of that firm is a personal friend of mine."

"I suppose you'll be going back to London tomorrow?"

"Yes, and I shall be starting at a godless hour in the morning. I have another car on my hands, a car lent to me by the Berkshire police, and as I've never learned to drive two cars at the same time I've got to leave this one with you."

Vincent returned to his hotel on foot. He spent the evening after dinner in marshalling his knowledge of shot wounds from cases in which he had helped police surgeons in their examinations of bodies that had met their deaths from revolver shots. He knew that there must have been at least two men in the car besides the murdered man, since the body had been lifted and not dragged into the barn. It was the body of a heavy man.

How had they been sitting? That was easy to determine. He had examined the body. There were two orifices in the head—one on the right side which was obviously the orifice of entrance, because its edges were torn and lacerated and blackened as if they had been burned by the heat and flame of the explosion. The orifice of exit on the left side was larger with its skin edges turned outward, and it was from this side of the car that the broken window had been taken, so the murdered man must have been sitting on the back seat of the car and his assailant must have been sitting beside him. The seat beside the driver might have been vacant. There was nothing to show this one way or the other. According to gangster phraseology, therefore, the victim must have been "taken for a ride."

But was suicide to be ruled out? A suicide practically always directs his weapon at what he knows to be a vital spot—the head or the heart—because he wishes to die swiftly and with the least possible suffering after the wound is inflicted.

The pistol is either dropped or, in one case that he remembered when he was a junior patrol in Soho, still grasped in the hand. But even if the pistol had been fired by the victim himself holding it in his right hand and pulling the trigger with his forefinger, the bullet would have had an upward tendency and the glass window would not have been shattered at the same horizontal level as the victim's head. All these facts went to show it was a case of murder and not suicide.

Chapter Three

VINCENT was on the road by five minutes to six the next morning, free to plan his next move. Clearly the first thing to do was to take Lindsay, the manager of Mendel's outfitting shop, down to Oldbury to identify the body of the murdered man if he could. There ought to be little difficulty about that, but there was another question. What would his superiors and his colleagues say about the escape from justice of two men who might have been detained on suspicion if he had arrived at Newquay in time. At the Yard there were always critics of chief inspectors who had climbed over the heads of older men and these would, of course, be busy. They would be saying that a more energetic and experienced officer would have done something towards getting the boat followed. That kind of critic doesn't bother himself about dates or timetables; all he looks to is success or failure. The boat had had two days' start when he took over the case; never mind, the critics would say, he ought to have found out more about her; he ought not to have left Newquay without discovering to what port she was going. But Vincent was not the kind of man to become a prey to misgivings. His own mind was clear about the course he should follow. The first thing to do was to get the identity of the murdered man established by some witness who knew him and Lindsay might turn out to be that witness.

As he had hoped, Vincent reached London in time to catch Lindsay on his return from lunch, having sent a message to Sergeant Walker to meet him near the outfitter's shop. His sergeant was pacing up and down, stopping at intervals to gaze at works of art displayed in a shop window, but he was quickly aware of the arrival of his superior. Vincent also seemed to be attracted by the statuary and the engravings. He pulled up opposite the shop window and jumped out to look at them.

"Follow me discreetly into the shop I'm going to," he said in a low voice as if he were addressing a bust of William Shakespeare.

He had previously telephoned to Lindsay to announce himself. He ran up the stairs to a little glazed office, from which his friend passed all his customers in review, and tapped on the window. Lindsay threw open the door and shook hands with his friend warmly.

"I'm always seeing your name in the papers, Vincent, and it's a pleasure to meet you again in the flesh."

"I'm afraid that when you hear the nature of my errand you will wish that you'd never seen or heard of me. I've come to ask you to run down with me to Oldbury."

"What for?"

"To identify, if possible, a murdered man. It may prove to be a wild goose chase, but here's an overcoat found in a car in which a murder was committed and it bears your firm's label."

Lindsay took the coat and became alert. "I sold this coat myself to a man whom we know quite well—a Mr Bernard

Pitt, one of our regular customers. Do you mean to say that he's been murdered?"

"Well, either that or he has murdered someone else."

Lindsay was shocked. "Bernard Pitt couldn't have been a murderer: he could only have been the victim."

"Can you describe him?"

"He was a biggish man, taller and broader than I am—between forty and fifty and growing bald; at any rate his hair was thin."

"That description fits the body exactly," said Vincent, "but so it would many other people. Can you tell me what was Mr Pitt's profession?"

"As it happens, I can. He was the Chief Accountant of the Asiatic Bank at its head office in Lombard Street. He let it out inadvertently one day."

"Have you his private address?"

"Yes, I have it noted somewhere. Here it is—7, Leicester Avenue, Hampstead. I've dined with him there more than once. It's a large house standing in its own garden, with a staff of manservants mostly foreign."

"That strikes me as peculiar—a bank cashier living in a style like that."

"I think he must have private means. Shall I ring up and ask whether he's at home now?"

"I wish you would."

Lindsay went to a telephone in another room and returned a few minutes later, saying: "The answer is that he left home on Saturday and hasn't yet returned. The servants don't know where he has gone."

"Saturday was the day of the murder. I fear that you'll have to come down with me to Oldbury to identify, or otherwise, this murdered man I've told you about. His body was discovered in a barn at Oldbury."

"When do you want me to come?"

"Immediately if you can arrange it."

"Very well, in a case like this I must arrange it, if you'll wait five minutes while I put the baby to bed. You'll find newspapers on that table."

Vincent scorned the newspapers and moved restlessly about the tiny room during the five minutes, while Sergeant Walker wrote stolidly in his notebook. Lindsay reappeared attired for a motor journey.

"This is the most exciting thing that has happened to me since I left the Service. Lead on."

Lindsay had looked forward to a brilliant career in the Navy, little suspecting that the Fates in the persons of certain hard-boiled naval officers at the Admiralty were poising an axe over his head. It had been a shock to him to find himself one of the many promising officers thrown out into a cold world with an inadequate gratuity, but he had made the best of it and had been glad to take over the management of an outfitter's shop.

Vincent's driving, careful though it was at crossroads, occasionally exceeded the speed limit for built-up areas. On reaching Oldbury they drove straight to Hatch, the village in which the barn was situated. The body had been removed to the village hall for identification.

"You'd better jump down, Walker, and get the key to the hall from that cottage opposite."

The sergeant returned two minutes later with the village constable, who carried the key in his hand. He stopped only to shoo off a bevy of small boys who were collecting to enjoy whatever spectacle there might be to boast about to their less fortunate schoolfellows.

The body was lying on a trestle table covered with a sheet borrowed from the local joiner and undertaker. The sheet was turned back and Lindsay recognized with a shock his former customer, Bernard Pitt, Chief Accountant in the Asiatic Bank.

They drove on to Oldbury to see Inspector Miller, to whom Vincent reported the identification.

"This is going to save us all a lot of work, Mr Vincent. Let me congratulate you," said the inspector.

"Thank you, but I can't help thinking that the work is only just beginning. We have to lose no time in trying to head off these rascals when they land in France or whatever country they may have been making for."

"The reporters have been worrying my life out. I suppose that now that the body has been identified we can give it out to the press. It would be very kind of you, Mr Vincent, if you would draft out something that I can get run off on a Roneo and give to the reporters."

"Certainly, Mr Miller. I should make the announcement quite short, yet sufficiently informative to justify you in saying that you have nothing to add to it—something like this." He tore a page out of his notebook and pencilled on it: "The police have now succeeded in identifying the body of the man which was found in a barn at Hatch during the thunderstorm last Saturday. It was the body of Mr Bernard Pitt, of 7, Leicester Avenue, Hampstead." "There! How will that do?"

"Excellent from my point of view, but not, I fear, from that of the reporters."

"Well, that's all they'll get for the present."

"I suppose that you yourself will lose no time in going there."

"My sergeant and I will go to the manager's private address this evening, so I shall be obliged if you will hold over your information to journalists until after the late editions are out and on sale."

"Certainly. The announcement shall not appear in the press until tomorrow morning."

"Good! If you are not in need of your car tomorrow it may be very useful to me."

"Certainly, you must keep it. It is a great relief to me that you have taken over the case and I have my chief constable's authority to lend you the official car for as long as you need it. For my part I shall give you every assistance that lies in my power."

The two officers shook hands warmly and Vincent resumed his seat at the wheel.

"Where shall I drop you?" asked Vincent. "At that shop of yours?"

"No; I've put the baby to bed. Why shouldn't we dine together and make a night of it?"

"Nothing doing. I've my hands full this evening."

"What a man! I tell you, I wouldn't take on your job for four times my present screw. No, give me the quiet, regular life of a shopkeeper with no watches to keep..."

"I haven't forgotten that you were once a naval officer and that presumably you must know a good deal about motorboats. Given a motorboat about twenty-five feet over all, could she safely cross the Channel to the French coast from north Cornwall?"

"That depends on the weather. In a calm sea of course she could. But why these intriguing questions?"

Vincent explained what had happened at Newquay and his companion frowned when he heard that the launch had no name. "That longshoreman with the foul clay pipe wasn't far wrong when he said that there was something crooked about that boat. I wonder what it was. But don't worry. You'll get to the bottom of it all right. You might put me down in St

James's Square. You'll know where to find me tomorrow if you want me."

As soon as Vincent had set down his passenger, Sergeant Walker took the vacant seat beside him, and he asked: "What did they say at the Lab about that broken window?"

"That the glass was perforated by a pistol bullet."

"As we thought. Well, now we have got to see the manager of the Asiatic Bank. We have his name from Lindsay, but it is after closing time. Here's a telephone box. Jump down and look up his address in the directory."

Sergeant Walker found the address without difficulty and they were fortunate enough to find the manager at home and at liberty to see them. The poor man listened gravely to what Vincent told him.

"I've been expecting this," he said. "I think that you will find that it was a case of suicide. For some time past the auditors have been working late hours at the bank—in fact they are there at this moment—and they have reason to believe that they have found evidence of extensive defalcations in the accounts, very cleverly carried out, but none the less capable of proof."

"Have you had suspicion about him for long?"

"No, only for about ten days or a fortnight. The discovery came as a great shock to the directors and to myself. He was entirely trusted and no doubt he had greatly extended the bank's business."

"What first made you suspect him?"

"I received an anonymous letter."

"Do you know anything about his private life?"

"No, not very much. He seemed to be living on a scale within his salary. He had a small flat in Bloomsbury."

"I may tell you confidentially that his tailor gave me a different address—that of a large house standing in its own grounds in Hampstead."

The manager stared at him aghast. "You mean that he was leading a double life?"

"Certainly the house of which I speak was costing him far more than his salary as your cashier would run to. He had a staff of menservants—mostly foreigners."

"Good Lord!...This will be a shock to the directors when they hear of it and I suppose that most of the blame will fall on me. Still, you'll have to tell them, of course, unless you leave me to do it and so save my face a little."

"I've only just started my enquiries; probably I shan't see the directors myself for a day or two and if you like to prepare them I shall have no objection at all. In any case it will be in all the papers tomorrow that he's been found murdered. It may even be in the stop press news tonight."

"Have you established the fact that it was a murder and not a suicide?"

"Only to my own satisfaction: the inquest has been adjourned."

Although it was obvious that the manager was bursting with questions to which he wanted answers, Vincent firmly took his leave.

His next visit was to the house in Hampstead. He waited in the car while Walker rang the bell: a deferential foreign butler or valet opened the door. The man had a startled look and Vincent caught a glimpse of a knot of other menservants huddled together at the top of the back stairs, listening. He guessed that they had already seen the stop press news in their dead master's evening paper.

Walker's first question was: "Can we see Mr Pitt?"

"He is not at home, sir."

"Indeed? When did he leave home?"

"On Saturday, sir."

"For long?"

"I do not think he will come back ever. If you wish I will show you the evening paper."

"You mean that he is dead?"

"Yes sir."

Walker turned towards the car. "It did get out in the stop press news: these people all know about it."

Vincent alighted quickly and addressed the man at the door. "Are you Mr Pitt's butler?"

"Yes sir."

"Well, I am a chief inspector from Scotland Yard and I have come to lock up and seal the rooms containing his property and also to take down the names of you and your staff."

"Will you come in, gentlemen?"

"Where is the dining room? I will see you all in there."

The man threw open a door on the right. "This is the dining room, sir."

At a sign from his chief, Walker sat down at the highly polished table and took out writing materials. The room was very expensively furnished; it was obviously far beyond the means of a bank cashier.

"Your name, please," said Walker.

The man gave a name that sounded like a sneeze and Walker asked him to write it down. Instead he produced the envelope of a letter on which the name and address were clearly inscribed. While Walker was copying this the man said: "You need not call me by those names. Everybody know me as 'Anton.' The postman also, he know me by that name."

"Well, Anton, how long have you been here in Mr Pitt's service?"

"About ten months. I come in September last year."

"When did you enter the country?"

"Just after the war. I was treated as ally. I served many distinguished noblemen. I have all my references upstairs. Shall I show them to you?"

"Later we will see them, but now I want you to bring in the other servants one by one and act as our interpreter."

"Very good, sir."

Anton proved to be an efficient master of ceremonies, though his manner of proceeding might not have satisfied a Master of the Household. His summons to his subordinates was a snap of the fingers reinforced by a whistle through the teeth and the hissing of a name. One by one his myrmidons were brought in. Their names and duties were recorded by Sergeant Walker, and not one of them omitted to mention the amount of wages due to him. When the list was complete this question of wages became acute.

"The police cannot pay your wages, nor provide you with lodgings for the night. You may remain in the house for the time being, but you must not attempt to enter any of the rooms that are locked."

Vincent then dismissed all the servants except Anton, telling them that they were free to come and go and to seek other employment. To Anton he said: "I'm going to leave you in charge of the house. You must not admit anyone without first ringing me up at Scotland Yard—Whitehall 1212. Now, I want you to answer a few questions. Did your master leave this house alone, or had he a friend with him?"

"He went alone, just as he did when going to his office and at the same hour."

"Did he go by car?"

"No sir; he went never to his office in the car. That stop here till the evening and he did not take it out often in the evening and never on Saturday because the chauffeur always had the day off."

"Did he ever drive himself?"

"No sir; he always had the chauffeur: you have seen him."

"When your master left on Saturday, did he say that he would be away for some time?"

"No, he said nothing. Always on Saturday he give dinner party and Francis he did the marketing on Saturday and prepare as usual."

"Now, Anton, I want you to think carefully before you answer my next question. Did any lady or gentleman call here and ask to see him last Friday—the day before he left home?"

"Yes, two gentlemen dined with him here."

"Were they English?"

"Oh yes."

"Had they ever been here before?"

"Oh yes; often."

"What were their names?"

"Mr Blake and Mr Lewis."

"Can you describe them?"

"Mr Blake he was very big and heavy, and Mr Lewis he was tall, too, but thin, and he looked older than Mr Blake."

"Now, Anton, I want to see every room in the house. We must see that there is a key to every room and we must put a label on each key."

"I have no labels, sir."

"No, but this officer has them. He will go with you round the rooms, lock them up, label the key and bring it down to this room. As you are all anxious about your wages, I advise you to apply to the Home Office tomorrow morning and there you will find that I have reported your case, too. They will tell you what to do."

When all the rooms were locked and the keys stowed in Sergeant Walker's bag, Vincent gave Anton his final instructions.

"You quite understand, you must admit no one before I come here tomorrow morning. They can wait if they please until I come, but they must not move beyond the hall. If you have any trouble with one of them, ring up the number I have given you and ask for me—Chief Inspector Vincent."

Chapter Four

VINCENT and Walker arrived at the house in Hampstead at nine o'clock the next morning. Anton admitted them. He had the appearance of a man who had slept ill.

"You look at if you'd spent a disturbed night," said Vincent.

"Sir, I have no sleep at all. These journalists they are terrible. They keep me up answering the telephone till after two this morning and then because I will tell them no more than your communiqué, they come round and ring the bell. When I tell them to go to Scotland Yard they become angry."

"In your case I should not answer the bell or the telephone."

"Then, sir, they start knocking and keep on knocking. No one can sleep when that knocker is going rat-tat-tat..."

Walker produced his bag of keys and the officers began their search in the library. Not a single letter or paper of any kind was found in the desk or in the drawers. Vincent rang the bell and Anton appeared.

"Go and bring me the man whose duty it is to clean this room, and stay here with us to act as interpreter."

"Yes sir, but that man speaks English very well."

"Bring him in then."

Anton returned with an upstanding young man with an open face. He was a Serbian and a fluent linguist.

"You clean this room every morning?"

"Yes sir."

"Before your master left the house on Saturday did you find burnt papers in the grate?"

"Yes sir, for many days last week the grate was full of burnt paper."

"Just letters or bigger documents?"

"Both, sir, but mostly letters."

"Did you notice anything else remarkable in the room when you cleaned it on Saturday morning?"

"Only that I think my master had been studying late on Friday night. There were books everywhere—on the table, on the chairs and even on the floor. Some were open, some closed."

"And you put them all back tidily in their shelves? Can you remember which books they were?"

"Some of them, sir. I will show you some that I remember."

He brought down from the shelf three or four books which Vincent examined with curiosity. They were all in quarto size, but they varied greatly in their subjects—history, biography, travel and science. In one respect they were alike, there was a note in figures on the flyleaf—a pencilled note such as (to quote the first three) 797, 1325, 410.

Having dismissed the manservant, Vincent turned to Walker. "What do you make of these figures? They must mean something."

"A code, do you think?"

Vincent shook his head. "I remember hearing in France that when a certain statesman died and his effects came to be examined they found that he was apparently penniless, until someone had the inspiration to flutter the leaves of one of the books in his library and out slid a thousand-franc note. This led to a systematic search in the books and it was found that a fortune was thus hoarded in his library. Needless to say that this statesman was foremost in the cry, 'defend the franc.' He was the great opponent of devaluation."

"You think, then, that these figures represent amounts of money hoarded in each book. But they are such odd numbers."

"Not if the greater part of them consisted in treasury notes which cannot be traced."

"Then you think that the owner was absconding with a large sum?"

"I think it is very probable. This is a large house; probably Pitt entertained friends here a good deal. We'll get Anton in again and ask him. Call him, will you?"

Anton crossed the hall almost at a run. "Yes sir?"

"Did Mr Pitt entertain friends here to dinner or lunch?"

"Not to lunch, sir, but to dinner—oh yes. He had very important people to dinner—people with titles. And François, the chef here, is very noted for his cooking."

"How often did your late master give dinner parties?"

"Quite once a week, sir, and sometimes oftener—always on Saturdays."

"Were there ladies among his guests?"

"No sir; only gentlemen."

"They played cards, of course, after dinner."

"Yes sir, always. There were four card tables set out upstairs."

"Mr Blake and Mr Lewis—were they always present at these parties?"

"Yes sir, always, and I think they used to win a good deal of money."

"Why do you think that?"

"Well, sir, Mr Pitt used to come down with them to the door, while I held it open and helped them to put on their coats and I heard Mr Pitt say: 'You've been lucky again to-night. I hope you won't frighten all my guests away!'" Anton seemed to plume himself upon having given some useful information.

"Did your master dine out in the evening sometimes?"

"Oh, yes sir, very often."

"And the chauffeur will remember where he went for dinner?"

"Yes sir. Shall I call him?"

"Yes, please."

The chauffeur was an Englishman, specially chosen, thought Vincent, for his taciturnity. He stood to attention with his cap in his hand waiting to be questioned.

"How long have you been in Mr Pitt's service?"

The man appeared to be embarked upon mental arithmetic, using the fingers of his left hand for his calculations.

"About ten months."

"Was the car a new one when you took it over?"

"Yes sir, I took it from the makers and, of course, it had to be run in."

"Did your master use it much?"

"Not very much; he used it in the evening for short runs in the town to take him out to dinner and sometimes on a Sunday to take friends to Brighton."

"Where did he usually dine when he went out?"

"At different houses."

"And clubs?"

"Only at one club—the Ace of Hearts in Piccadilly."

"Did you have to wait for him to bring him back?"

"No, he would tell me the time to fetch him, and generally he did not keep me waiting."

"Can you remember the addresses of any people with whom he used to dine most frequently?"

"Mr Brooklyn in Jermyn Street, number seventy-one—that was one place."

"Do you mean that he went there more frequently than to any other house?"

"Yes, he never missed a week without going there."

"Thank you. This one address will do for the present. On Saturday morning when he went away, had he given you no orders?"

"He told me I could take the day off."

"Did you always have the day off on Saturday?"

"No, not always. He often went out on Saturday evening."

"But Anton tells me he always gave dinner parties on Saturday."

"Oh, sir—these foreigners they lose count of days."

"Well, you know that you have to look for another job and that we are going to lock up the garage? You can all stay here for a day or two while you are looking for another place. I may want to see you again later in the day."

Having dismissed the chauffeur, Vincent rose. "Now, Walker, I think that our next visit should be to 71, Jermyn Street. At this hour probably we shall find the gentleman at home."

As Vincent had surmised, Mr Brooklyn proved to be a gentleman of leisure, and as far as he was able to judge from the furnishings of his flat, a gentleman of ample means. Vincent sent his card up by the man-servant who opened the door. Mr Brooklyn appeared to be tickled at receiving a visit from a prominent officer of the Criminal Investigation Department and he received Vincent with cordiality.

"The blow has fallen at last," was his greeting. "I knew that some day my sins would find me out and I was wondering which of them would first bring me into the meshes of the law." He sank his voice to a portentous whisper. "Is it about that woman I threw into the canal? Or the gentleman in Battersea Park from whom I demanded money with menaces? I shall plead guilty to both of them. You've brought the handcuffs with you, of course. I should not like my manservant to miss any of the fun."

The man was good-looking and younger than Vincent had expected. He smiled.

"On this occasion, Mr Brooklyn, I have only a question or two to ask you with, of course, the usual caution that your replies will be taken down in writing and may be used. But seriously, I have come to ask for any information you can give me about the late Mr Pitt."

"The *late* Mr Pitt?"

"Surely you have read in the paper about the finding of Mr Pitt's body in a barn at Hatch in Berkshire?"

"To tell you the truth, I haven't opened the paper yet: I breakfast late."

"Well, it was in the stop press last night. Do you know the Christian name of your friend?"

"No, I don't. All I know is that he signed his letters 'B. Pitt.'"

"Well, we have strong reason to believe that your friend was the cashier of the Asiatic Bank. Had you any idea of that?"

Brooklyn drew in his breath with a whistling sound. "He was leading a double life, you mean— the man about town in his lighter moments, and the hard-working bank official when he felt like work. I should never have thought it, nor would you if you had known him."

"When did you see him last?"

"I dined at his house one day last week. He was in the best of health and spirits then."

"Were you his only guest on that occasion?"

"No, there were half a dozen of us."

"And among them a Mr Lewis and a Mr Blake?"

"The two Americans, you mean? Yes, they were there."

"They were Americans? And after dinner you played cards?"

"We did. I shan't easily forget that card party. Those two Yanks skinned me alive."

"Really, it is about those two men that I am trying to get information. Can you by any chance tell me their address?"

"When I last saw them I gave them a lift home to their hotel—the Carlton."

"Thank you, Mr Brooklyn, that is what I wanted —their address."

"At the risk of seeming indiscreet I confess that it would interest me to know what sort of crime they are wanted for. Cheating at cards would be my guess." Vincent laughed. "I'm afraid that it would be premature to say whether your guess is right or wrong. Thank you very much for seeing me."

It was but a step for the two police officers to reach the Carlton. There they drew blank; neither of the two names was known.

"I'm not surprised," said Vincent to his colleague. "This is not the kind of hotel they would affect. If it had been the Globe…"

"Do you think that Mr Brooklyn was lying?" asked Walker.

"No, I think that they were putting him off the scent. Now, Walker, you took down from the bank manager the address of the rooms in Bloomsbury which Pitt had given as his lodgings."

Walker took out his notebook and read: "12, Redcliff Street, W.C.2."

"Come along then. We'll pick up the car and try our luck there."

At 12, Redcliff Street, they had better luck than they expected. Mr Pitt, they learned, had occupied rooms there, also his two American friends, Mr Lewis and Mr Blake.

The landlady received them in a little room which she called "my office." She seemed quite glad to exercise her tongue and not in the least anxious lest it should carry her too far.

"Of course I read this morning about the murder of a Mr Pitt, but I didn't know it was my Mr Pitt, although it set me wondering; you see it gave the dead gentleman's address in a big house in Hampstead, but I suppose the police do sometimes make mistakes. You're sure it was *my* Mr Pitt?"

"Quite sure."

"Then I'll tell you something. If you ask me, Mr Pitt's body isn't the only one you'll find. There are two more of my lodgers missing. Ah! I see you didn't know that."

"You mean Mr Lewis and Mr Blake?"

"How did you know? Have their bodies been found already?"

"No."

"Oh, you'll find them all right if you look about. They all went off together last Saturday and not a word heard from them since."

"Did they say they were coming back?"

"Oh yes, they were as happy as schoolboys going on a holiday—all went off in the car together."

"Did they take much luggage?"

"Mr Blake and Mr Lewis did, but you see Mr Pitt didn't have any here since he had to sleep at his old mother's house to keep her company."

"Do you know where his mother lived?"

"Out north, I believe, but I couldn't tell you the address."

"How long has he lived here altogether?"

"About four years and it's only for the last twelve months or less that he hasn't slept here."

"Why did he still keep on his rooms?"

"Well, he had lunch here every day and had letters sent here and was always thinking his mother would get better and that he would come back."

"Well, now, Mrs Briggs, we want to look round the rooms of these three missing men beginning with those of Mr Lewis and Mr Blake."

"They had a nice little flat on the second floor—two bedrooms and the sitting room they shared. Perhaps you'd like to start with those."

"Well, we needn't trouble you now any longer. We have to make it a rule to do our searching alone. In ten minutes or so we will call you."

The search they conducted was as thorough as long practice could make it. The underside of every drawer was scrutinized and the paper linings were taken out; but nothing was found.

"It is quite evident that these fellows meant to bolt," said Vincent. He opened the door and found Mrs Briggs hovering about on the landing outside, bursting with curiosity.

"I suppose you won't tell me whether you've found anything," she said archly.

"No, Mrs Briggs; I can tell you quite truthfully that we've found nothing, but you'll find that we've put everything back tidily in its place."

"You'll find that I can be trusted, gentlemen. Just now while you were in that room a reporter called and I never let on that you were here."

"Quite right, Mrs Briggs. Who did the motor car belong to that your lodgers went away in—Mr Blake or Mr Lewis?"

"I understand from what they told me that they'd hired it for a week."

"Do you know what garage they hired it from?"

"No, I don't, but there are three or four round here where you can hire a car."

"Well, now we would like to see Mr Pitt's rooms."

"Yes, they're on the first floor—a sitting room and bedroom opening into one another."

She led the way downstairs and opened the door facing them. "You'll excuse their not being quite tidy, but we were leaving it till the day before he was to come back. There's a lot of burnt paper in the grate..."

"So I see," said Vincent. "Well, now I fear that you must leave us to our work. We shan't be longer over it than we can help."

Walker went first to the fireplace and turned over the carbonized paper. "The ashes have all been chawed up," he said; "it's no good saving any of them for expert examination."

A search of the drawers in the writing table produced nothing. There remained only the wardrobe in which were hanging three suits of clothes, not bearing the name of the Sackville Street tailor. They bore signs of hard use.

Vincent went through the pockets with a practised hand, but found them empty until he came to the third jacket. This also he was about to restore to its hanger when he thought that he heard rather than felt the crackle of paper. Again he plunged his hand into the breast pocket, which he had already explored without result. This time his fingers came upon a thin sheet of paper pressed close against the pocket lining. He took it out. It was a milliner's bill from the Maison Germaine in the rue Duphot, Paris. It was charged to Monsieur Pitt. There was but one item, "*Chapeaux*, 100,000 francs."

"What," asked Vincent, "could Mr Pitt be doing with a hundred thousand francs' worth of ladies' hats?"

Chapter Five

WALKER WAS ASTONISHED to see his chief suddenly take three rapid turns round the room, kicking the furniture impatiently out of his way. Then he halted and handed the bill to his sergeant.

"What do you make of that, Walker?"

Walker shook his head in token that the solution was beyond him.

"It seems to me," said Vincent, "that a visit to Paris by one of us is foreshadowed. Hats might mean anything except hats. Yes, one of us or both will have to cross the Channel and make the acquaintance of Madame Germaine in the rue Duphot."

"There is the language difficulty, Mr Vincent. I don't speak French, but, of course, you do. It won't be the first job that you have undertaken across the Channel."

"My French is traveller's French, The natives over there are too polite to smile at it, but generally they require me to repeat my question and they wear a pained expression when they listen to it. Still, I'm convinced that we must know something more about Madame Germaine than we do now. It's possible that we might run into the two gentlemen that we want to interview. But the first thing to do is to make a round of the garages in this quarter and trace the people who let out that car on hire. You have the date and the number of the car, so we'll take our leave and divide the work of making the enquiries between us."

It was Vincent who first found the garage that owned the car, and when the young woman in the glazed box learned the nature of the enquiry she seized her telephone and rang up a number in excited tones.

"If you'll wait a minute, sir, the proprietor himself will come down. He was just thinking of acquainting Scotland Yard, because the gentleman that signed for the car has been found murdered; we read it in the paper."

A man whose gait indicated haste entered the garage with a proprietary look about him.

"What's all this?" he asked the young woman.

"This gentleman is from Scotland Yard. He's called about that sixteen-horse Daimler hired by Mr B. Pitt."

"What I want to know is where is my car and how can I get it back?" he said to Vincent anxiously.

"I can answer your first question. It is in the hands of the police at Newquay, and your best plan would be to ring them up on the telephone. The window was broken by a revolver shot and a new window was put in at the expense of the men who hired it. And now that I have answered your question I will ask you some of my own. What were the men like who hired your car?"

"There were three of them. Mr Pitt, who signed for the car, said that he was cashier in the Asiatic Bank, Lombard Street, and I verified this on the telephone. He had two men with him; I think they were Americans by their accent."

"Was one of them broad and heavily built and the other an older man, tall and thin?"

"Yes, you've described them exactly."

"How long did they hire the car for?"

"They said they wanted it for the inside of a week and so I let it to them by the day."

"Well, I should lose no time in telephoning to the police at Newquay to find out when you can have your car back. I suppose you made them pay a deposit?"

"Did I not? That's the rule with everyone who hires a car, unless he's personally known to me, and Mr Pitt was not."

"In what form did Mr Pitt make his deposit with you?"

"In treasury notes. Thirty pounds was the amount of the deposit. To tell you the truth I didn't much like the look of those two Americans. They seemed to be slippery customers somehow, and if it comes to that, Pitt himself was a queer fish. What had a bank cashier to do with a big house full of foreigners up in Hampstead? I suppose you could tell me something about that."

"What I'm concerned with is to find the murderer," said Vincent, ignoring the last remark. "Can you remember anything that would be likely to help me—for example any conversation between the three men?"

"No, but after they'd gone a man came in; he said that he had a garage and that the three men had been round to him but that he didn't have a car smart enough for them. He asked me what kind of car I'd lent them and I told him; that was all."

"He didn't say where his garage was?"

"No, he didn't. I'd never seen him before, but there are lots of little garages about here."

Vincent decided that for the moment it was not worth while to hunt up this second garagist. He thanked the man and left, hoping to head off his sergeant. To his relief he saw him coming down the street.

"It's all right, Walker: this is where the car was hired and the description of the men tallies with the description of the fellows who embarked from Newquay. I shall have to see Mr Richardson and let him decide the step that ought to be taken. While I'm at the Central Office you might make it your job to find out whether those two rascals have registered as aliens. The landlady gave you their initials."

"Yes, I have them: G. Lewis and R. Blake. I'll be off now." Chief Constable Richardson was startled when his messenger announced that Chief Inspector Vincent wanted to see him.

"I thought that the chief inspector had been lent to the Berkshire constabulary. Well, show him in." Vincent presented himself and Richardson looked up. "I thought you were down in the wilds of Berkshire, or was it Cornwall?"

"Both, sir," replied Vincent, with a smile, "but my enquiries indicate two Americans as having been guilty of murder in this country. In order to get further evidence I am asking your leave to go over to Paris."

"To Paris? I'm rather out of touch with what you've been doing. Before I authorize you to go so far afield I think you had better give me a verbal resumé of the case as far as you have got in it."

Vincent had a gift for terse narrative. He omitted nothing from his story and yet he reduced it to reasonable length.

"You didn't yourself see the motor launch at Newquay?"

"No sir."

"And yet you are satisfied that it could cross the Channel even in rough weather without danger?"

"I had to depend on what the sailors at Newquay said about her, but they satisfied me that she was a safe sea boat and I gathered that they were competent judges."

"One has to be careful or the Receiver may get on his hind legs. All the expenses you have incurred for the Berkshire constabulary now come out of the Metropolitan Police Fund, and if we add your expenses abroad without special authority, he may have a good deal to say. Why not go and explain the case personally to him, saying that I have sent you."

"Very good, sir, I will."

"You may quote me as saying that personal enquiry in the country itself is a secret of success in cases like this. He will remember that it was in this way that I succeeded in clearing up two of our biggest cases."

The man who had come from the Home Office as Receiver was no dry-as-dust accountant. On the contrary he was keenly interested in police work and ready to make any concessions that seemed likely to bring about success. In the hands of Vincent the story was convincing: it was evident that without this visit to Paris the ship would be spoiled for a ha'porth of tar, but when Vincent suggested taking a subordinate with him he drew the line.

"I can quite understand your case, Chief Inspector, that when you are making enquiries you must have someone with you to do the fetch and carry jobs in a big case, but to take a sergeant, ignorant of French, across the Channel would be in my opinion an indefensible waste of money. If you find it necessary to go, you'll have to go alone."

"Very good, sir," said Vincent with a sigh. He returned to Richardson's room and was fortunate enough to find him alone.

"Well?" asked his chief, looking up with keen eyes. "Did you melt the hard heart of the Receiver?"

"No sir, but he was very nice about it. I'm sure that he would have given way if he could. I can go over to France myself, but I cannot take a junior officer with me. Happily I'm on very good terms with an officer of the Sûreté with whom I worked during the war."

"That's all right then. You can go over to Paris as soon as you like; in fact the sooner the better. While you are there you had better call upon two friends of mine, M. Bigot and M. Verneuil, both of them members of the Paris police. They will remember having worked with me and I trust you to give them the usual friendly messages."

Vincent found Sergeant Walker waiting for him at the basement entrance. There was an expectant look on his face which his chief dispelled by a shake of the head.

"Nothing doing for you, my friend. I have to go alone to save expenses."

"That's all right, Mr Vincent. I was never one for foreign travel. You look such a fool in a country where you don't even know how to ask for a light for your pipe. The good old Metrop is where I belong. I've made enquiry about those two men: they didn't register."

"All the better for us, because if they show up here again we shall have something to hold them on."

"Another thing I've found out is that the passport carried by the dead man had been tampered with. According to the Foreign Office records it had been issued to Bernard Pitt and the name had been obliterated with chemicals and 'John Whitaker' had been substituted."

"I know the stuff they use; they employed it a lot during the war. It will take out ink from any document without leaving a trace. Well, keep your eyes open while I'm away and if you hear anything that I ought to know, write to me at the Hotel du Louvre. I'll write it down for you. I ought to be back at latest in two days."

It chanced that during the war Vincent had had to work with a very intelligent and well-educated French commissary of police named Goron, who had lately married. They had since kept up a desultory correspondence and the Gorons had invited Vincent to come over and enjoy their hospitality. It was certainly an opportunity, since a ladies' hat shop in the rue Duphot which demanded 100,000 francs for a hat was new to his experience. He telegraphed to his French friend to expect him on the following morning, and he crossed the Channel by the night boat. Arrived at St Lazare Station, he took a taxi to the little apartment in the rue St Georges and found a warm welcome from Goron and his wife, a lively little woman from Normandy, who spoke a pretty broken English. Goron spoke no language but his own.

"To what are we indebted for the pleasure of seeing you, my friend?" asked Goron.

"It's a long story," began Vincent in French that was fluent but not impeccable.

"Pardon," interrupted Jacqueline Goron; "we can have no long stories until you have been fortified by a cup of my coffee after your journey."

"I must explain," said her husband in a whisper that was intended to be overheard, "that the salic law does not hold good in this flat: it is ruled exclusively by a female sovereign."

"Be careful," admonished Jacqueline, shaking her forefinger at him; "or I will tell Monsieur Vincent home truths about you that you will not be able to contradict because you are too lazy to learn English. As for example…"

"Enough! I capitulate." He held up both hands above his head.

"Take care what you say, my friend," put in Vincent. "We must do nothing to offend Madame when I am so soon to beg her help. This is the only clue I have for solving the problem that has brought me over to Paris."

He showed them the milliner's bill from the Maison Germaine.

Goron knitted his brows over it. "Whatever this is for it is not a hat," he said emphatically.

"Don't be so positive, Edouard," protested his wife. "I have seen hats for which I would willingly give a hundred thousand francs if I had had them to give."

"The question is," said Vincent, "whether Madame will consent to go to that hat shop and see who is running it and what their real business is."

"I can answer for her that she will," said her husband. "The only danger is that Madame Germaine may bribe her with a new hat."

Jacqueline made no answer to this gibe; she was in deep thought. "*Ecoute,*" she said suddenly; "my plan is made. You, Edouard, will be loitering on the opposite pavement looking into shop windows or what you will. Monsieur Vincent will be standing irresolute at the corner of the rue St-Honoré. I shall enter the shop boldly to investigate and shall choose a hat—I need one—but before buying it I shall have to seek the approval of my husband who is waiting for me outside. He will accompany me to the shop to pay for my hat and draw his own conclusions about the saleswoman. This concluded, we shall walk together to the rue St-Honoré and Monsieur Vincent, posing as an Englishman exploring Paris, will ask us the way to the Invalides. We shall then show him the way and walk with him down the rue Cambon and give him our impressions. Does my plan please you?"

She was evidently so pleased with it herself that Vincent would not have dared to pour cold water on it, but her husband had something to say.

"Your plan is admirable with one exception. It is not necessary to buy a hat: you could take me over to the shop and I could declare that the hat doesn't suit you."

"But that would be a manifest statement. The hat I shall choose will be most becoming. We will start immediately."

They shared a taxi to the Boulevard Madeleine, where Jacqueline left the two men and walked down the street by herself looking for the Maison Germaine. She stopped for a moment to look in the window and then went in. The opening of the shop door rang a bell. The little shop itself was empty, but the persistent ringing of the bell until the door was closed brought from an inner room a tall, good-looking woman in the thirties, beautifully dressed and groomed. Jacqueline proceeded to business at once and pointed to a hat in the window and asked its price. The modest sum quoted convinced her that this was not the shop where vast sums were spent on hats. She detected a slight foreign accent in the saleswoman and asked whether she were English.

"I myself am learning English and I love to practice it," she explained.

"No," said the lady pleasantly. "I am Austrian and I speak no English."

By this time, Jacqueline had fitted the hat on her head before a glass and was given up to the strange ecstasy which takes possession of every well-dressed woman when she tries on becoming headgear with a competent saleswoman at her elbow. She felt a prick of conscience when she thought of her husband and his English friend waiting for her to come out full to the brim with information, and put a tentative question:

"Surely, you have not been here very long, madame. I have often passed down this street and I could not have failed to see the ravishing hats displayed in your window."

"I have been here six months."

"With such talent as yours, I feel sure that you will succeed—unless this lamentable crisis affects you."

"On the contrary, madame, the crisis aids me, for clients accustomed to pay five hundred francs for a hat are glad nowadays to come to me and be supplied with hats to their taste at a far more moderate figure."

Jacqueline was so much interested that she continued the conversation for her own satisfaction until the sight of her husband pacing up and down on the opposite pavement brought her back to realities with a start.

"Oh, there's my husband!" she exclaimed. "I cannot finally decide on a hat without his approval."

She ran down the street to Goron. "Madame Germaine herself is serving me. She's an Austrian and her hats are a revelation and so inexpensive. I'm quite sure she must be all right, but come and see for yourself."

They spent about twenty minutes in the shop, finally buying a hat at a quite moderate price, and Jacqueline walked proudly out wearing the new hat and leaving the old one to be sent home.

"Well," she asked her husband eagerly, "am I not right about her? Such an artist could not be a criminal."

"In my career," said Goron, "I have had to deal with ladies quite as disarming as your Austrian friend and found them steeped to the lips in duplicity. I agree with you that it is hard to believe that this one is not up to her face value, but we must join our English friend who is waiting for us yonder."

Chapter Six

HAVING acquainted Vincent with the experience of Jacqueline in the hat shop, Goron made a suggestion.

"I propose," he said, "that we send Jacqueline home in a taxi and that you and I visit the police of the eighth arrondissement to inquire about the status of Madame Germaine."

Vincent jumped at the suggestion and the two men betook themselves to the police office in the Exhibition building. They had one disappointment. Monsieur Bigot, the chief, was absent on holiday, but Monsieur Verneuil, who was acting for him, could be seen if the business was in any way urgent. They were ushered into the acting chief's room, who rose to receive them.

Verneuil had been a petty officer in the French navy. Exposure to the weather had permanently coloured his skin to mahogany. He had a strong sense of caustic humour and there was very little about the foibles of his countrymen and countrywomen that he did not know.

Goron introduced Vincent as a British colleague who had come to the French Sûreté for help.

"You are perhaps a colleague of my esteemed friend, Monsieur Richardson."

"Monsieur Richardson has climbed high," said Vincent. "He is now one of the chief officers of Scotland Yard."

"I am not surprised; he was one of those marked for promotion."

"I hear that your comrade, Monsieur Bigot, is absent. Has he also achieved his promotion?" asked Vincent.

"You have employed the exact word—achieved, monsieur. He has indeed achieved it, but if you think that it has made him happy and contented you will be mistaken. He has become a slave and a beast of burden."

"A slave? To whom?"

"To the most merciless of slave owners—the politicians. He bemoaned to me the other day that he can no longer call his soul his own. His duties now lie in the lobbies of the Chamber, and the very atmosphere in that building is poisoned with intrigue. Perhaps it is the same in your House of Commons, monsieur?"

Vincent smiled, without committing himself to a reply.

"However that may be, in Paris even Wagner's hero Parsifal, of whom the newspapers are talking, would have succumbed to temptation, not from beauteous maidens emerging from gigantic flower petals but from the corrupting influence of money since, after all, no sane man would seek election as a deputy unless there were something solid to be made out of it."

"Now, Monsieur Verneuil, let us talk business. We have come to ask to have the dossier of Madame Germaine, the Austrian milliner in the rue Duphot, examined."

"Nothing easier," replied Verneuil; "if those rascals of mine have kept their files up to date." He stamped on the floor with his heel. A hangdog police clerk stood wilting in the doorway. "I want the dossier of an Austrian milliner in the rue Duphot, a woman named Germaine."

"Very good, monsieur."

When the dossier was brought, Verneuil scanned the pages, with a whimsical air of surprise. "*Tiens*," he said, "not a word recorded against her. Madame Germaine is of course her professional name—she is Fräulein Kofler—an Austrian from Vienna."

"We on the other side of the Channel have nothing against her unless it be that she is selling hats on an almost incredible scale—to the tune of a hundred thousand francs to a single customer."

"You think that she was smuggling them into England? That, surely, would be a matter for your customs officers, not for us."

"The man who had the bill which I am going to show you was not at all the type of person who would be trading in women's hats."

"But can you say of any man that he would not trade in women's hats if he had a pretty woman friend?"

"Not to the tune of one hundred thousand francs."

Verneuil shrugged his shoulders. "Not being married I have no first-hand evidence to go upon, but I understand that if a woman were condemned to change her hat ten times a day she would gladly forfeit her chance of eternal salvation. May I see this bill for one hundred thousand francs?"

Vincent put the bill into his hand. Verneuil scrutinized both the handwriting and the paper.

"Here is a bill my wife received from Madame Germaine this morning," said Goron.

Verneuil spread both bills out upon the table and compared them. "They are not in the same handwriting. *Tenez*, my friend, I myself will call on Madame Germaine and ask her the meaning of this large quantity of hats sold to England. Unless I am much mistaken, she will tell me that she knows nothing about it. If you gentlemen have no objection I will go alone and report to you afterwards the result of my enquiry."

"There is one other service that you might do for me, monsieur," said Vincent. "It is to ascertain whether two Americans—G. Lewis and R. Blake— have taken out cards of identity at any time."

"Nothing easier; I can give you that information from the telephone." He picked up his receiver and called a number. "Verneuil speaking. It concerns two Americans, G. Lewis and R. Blake." He spelt out the names. "Have they taken out cards of identity at any time? Ring me when you have the information."

He replaced the receiver and looked triumphantly at Vincent as who should say: "You see how wonderfully things are organized on *this* side of the Channel." While the telephone was being used Vincent had a brain wave. He knew that the road to a Frenchman's heart was down his throat. He would ask Verneuil to meet him and Goron for lunch and let him choose his pet restaurant. As he had expected, the ex-petty officer turned detective accepted with alacrity.

"This falls well, monsieur. I shall have seen Madame Germaine and can make my report to you over the *hors d'oeuvres*."

The telephone bell began to tinkle. Verneuil took up the receiver and then turned to Vincent and said, not without pride in his tone: "Two Americans— Rupert Blake and George Lewis—took out cards of identity in the fifteenth arrondissement last January. Their address at that time was 9, rue Violet. There, my friend, our system may not be perfect but at any rate it works."

"Thank you, monsieur; that information may be very useful to me. And now we will say 'au revoir' until twelve-thirty, when we meet at your pet restaurant near the Quai d'Orsay."

As the two friends left the office, Goron said: "We are in luck, my friend. That restaurant Verneuil is taking us to is kept by the ex-*maître d'hotel* of a cardinal famous for his cuisine. Now I must go and make my peace with Jacqueline and get her permission to lunch out."

"And I must return to my hotel to make myself fit to be seen. I came straight to you this morning from the boat train."

Vincent, looking immaculate, was the first to arrive at the restaurant, where he was received with ceremony by the proprietor who, as he remarked later, treated him as he would have treated a foreign diplomatist with a string of titles before his name. Goron, with meticulous punctuality, was close on his heels; Verneuil was ten minutes late and they sat down at their reserved table to wait for him. He came bursting in full of apologies.

"You will forgive me when I tell you the cause. I was right when I said that in my opinion that milliner knew nothing about that extravagant bill."

"You mean that someone must have stolen one of her bill-heads?"

"So she said. She assured me that she had no export trade with England, that being a great admirer of your country she often wished that she had, though not to the extent suggested by this invoice because that would mean employing hands in a factory to cope with it."

"Had she any suggestion to make about how one of her billheads could have been abstracted?"

"She said that nothing could be easier. The customer would merely ask to see a model from the window and while she had her back turned, an invoice could be taken from the desk where there are always several lying ready. She said that none of her customers spend that amount of money even in a year."

"The question before us," said Goron, "is what could have been the object of sending a bogus invoice to England if the hats were not to be supplied." Vincent pondered. "Two possibilities suggest themselves to me; the first that the invoice was intended to cover a sum of money that had been used for other purposes than hats; the second that it was to conceal the true nature of merchandise of another kind." Verneuil's eyes narrowed. "I think that the second of your explanations will prove to be the true one."

"But we have not yet dismissed the first possibility," said Goron; "that the invoice was intended to cover a sum of money that had been used for other purposes. My wife has a Spanish friend, a lady with a rich husband. She told her that Spanish husbands, however well to do, dislike handing over money to their wives, but that such is their love of outward show that they like their wives to be better dressed than other women and will cheerfully pay extravagant sums to their wives' dressmakers and milliners. The wives require money to indulge their little weaknesses, so they enter into an unholy alliance with the dressmaker or milliner, who charges the husband an exorbitant price and when he settles the bill the two, that is the wife and her milliner, divide the surplus between them."

"*Tiens!*" said Verneuil. "I did well to remain a bachelor. All the same, Madame Germaine has all her goods plainly priced and it would be difficult to deceive a French husband. What is the position in your country, Monsieur Vincent?"

"You must not ask me, for I, too, like you, am still a bachelor and know nothing about the expedients of married ladies who are kept short of cash."

"Well," said Goron, "as the meeting has decided against the first proposition by a majority, let us turn to the second; that this invoice covered other merchandise than hats."

"Now," said Verneuil, "we are upon the fringe of the truth. What merchandise can run into those figures? There is only one."

Goron, with a quick movement of his thin, lithe body, turned upon him. "You mean drugs?" Verneuil nodded significantly without speaking. "Then, Vincent, my friend, I must warn you that you have before you the most difficult case in your career."

Goron's excitement was infectious. Vincent, himself on wires, caught some of it. "Then all the more fun in solving it."

"That's the spirit! We'll have the fun of solving it together." They shook hands.

An amused smile curved Verneuil's lips. "It is easy to see that you two have preserved your youth."

"You see," explained Goron, "we were opposite numbers as intelligence officers on the French and British general staffs during the war, and my friend will agree with me that we worked together like brothers."

"Ah. Then you had what you call your fun even in those tragic days?"

"Yes, if you call it fun to be obsessed with the weight of responsibility for every bit of information we supplied to our chiefs."

For the rest of the meal Verneuil was content to remain a listener as the two younger men "swapped yarns" about their service nearly twenty years before. When they had no further excuse for lingering, Vincent said:

"I think that as Monsieur Verneuil has been good enough to find me the former address of those two Americans, I ought to go to the rue Violet this afternoon."

"Then I'll come with you," said Goron; "in a case like this, when American gangsters—is not that the word?—are concerned, two are better than one." Having arranged to report the result of their expedition to Verneuil a little later, the two friends hailed a taxi.

"Tell me," said Goron when they had given the address to the driver, "what type of man was this in whose room that invoice was found."

"He was the cashier of an important bank in London. It is now known that for many months he had been robbing his employers, and the day came when he thought it more prudent to abscond abroad, but he was murdered on the journey."

"*Tiens!* Then you have indeed a problem. Hats and bank securities. At first sight they seem ill-assorted. It will be a problem after my own heart."

"And according to Verneuil, drugs must not be ruled out."

"Ah! Verneuil has been working at the drug business a good deal and it threatens to become an obsession with him. It is well that we go together to the rue Violet, because I shall be able to extract more from the concierge and the chambermaid than you would as a foreign police officer."

The concierge proved to be a woman who had a constitutional dislike of betraying her lodgers to the police. As a concierge she was not a moral censor. Gentlemen brought their wives to lodge there, or they lodged alone. If they changed their wives occasionally what was that to her provided that they paid their bills?

Goron had drawn conclusions from her accent, though her colloquial French was fluent.

"You are not a Frenchwoman?"

"Sir, I have lived here for the greater part of my life; my sympathies are French to the core."

"That may be, but you have your card of permission to work in France?"

"I can show it to you, monsieur: there is not a mark on it against me."

"That may be, but let me remind you that a foreigner who declines to give necessary information to the police runs a risk…"

The woman's manner changed; she began to cringe. "Will you gentleman give yourselves the trouble of passing into my little room?" She threw open a door at the back of her glazed box and ushered them into a tiny cubicle of a room spotlessly clean and neat. "Doubtless Monsieur has come to make inquiries on the part of some husband, or it may be of some wife."

Vincent was about to make a disclaimer when Goron touched him on the sleeve.

"These two gentlemen did not stay here unaccompanied, I think?"

"Oh no; each of them brought his wife, or at any rate a lady companion."

"Were the ladies known as Madame Lewis and Madame Blake? I presume they had no letters, but they may have received parcels from shops. Were these parcels addressed 'Madame Lewis' and 'Madame Blake', respectively?"

"Certainly, monsieur."

Vincent had been a little impatient of his colleague's line of questioning, since the women seemed to him negligible, but now he began to see whither they were leading.

"Now," pursued Goron. "Let me have a description of each of these ladies. Madame Lewis, was she a Frenchwoman, smart and well dressed?"

The woman became voluble and assured them that both ladies were beautiful and very smart; their husbands were generous: that one could judge; probably they were not Frenchwomen, at any rate one of them was reading a Russian newspaper one day.

"I myself am a Russian, monsieur, and so I know."

"When were they last here?"

"In February." (She consulted a ledger.) "On February 23rd."

"Did you hear where they were going when they left?"

"No, monsieur, they all went away together in the same taxi. I can give you the address of the taxi driver, it was the man whom I always employ for my lodgers."

"Has he a particular rank for his taxi?"

"No, monsieur; he plies for hire privately and when he is not out with a fare, one finds him at home."

Vincent put his first question: "When ladies leave your rooms there are cardboard boxes and wrapping paper to clear away. For example, did these ladies leave hatboxes?"

"Every kind of box; as I tell you the husbands were generous."

"And you put the boxes with the rubbish of the house to be cleared away?"

"Not all, monsieur. Here is a box superior to the ordinary run and I've kept it for storing my papers." She brought forward a cardboard box.

Goron took it from her and pointed significantly to the address printed on the lid. Vincent read the words: "Germaine, rue Duphot, Paris."

Chapter Seven

GORON LOOKED at the address of the taxi driver and pronounced it to be within easy walking distance.

"That interview was not entirely barren, I think," he said as they walked.

"Indeed it was not. Either of those women might have been a customer of Madame Germaine and might have abstracted the bill-head of the note for one hundred thousand francs. I suppose that it will be possible to trace them?"

"If they registered as the law requires, it would be a matter of only a few minutes, but with foreigners engaged in shady business it may not be so easy. Some of them are very clever and we have only the names of their reputed husbands to go upon. If they were not legally married they would have registered under their maiden names which we don't know."

"The next question is whether a taxi driver would remember the address to which he drove people last February; it will be surprising if he does."

The taxi driver, as it appeared, lived on the fifth floor of a house without a lift. The concierge explained that orders for his taxi were telephoned to her and that she received a small commission on the fares he charged, for his taxi was to all intents a private carriage which did not ply for hire and was therefore not registered with the police: the proprietor charged what he liked. Fortunately the man was at home and he was gifted with a remarkable memory. He recalled without having to consult any diary that at the beginning of the last week in February he drove the American gentlemen and their wives from the rue Violet to St Lazare Station. They had with them suitcases, but no heavy luggage; he was glad to note this because they had been good clients of his and the absence of heavy luggage implied that they were crossing to England only for a few days.

"Did they return?" asked Goron.

"No, monsieur; they talked of returning, but they cannot have come to this district, otherwise they would have employed me."

"You say they were good clients?"

"Yes, monsieur; not a day passed without their telephoning for me; all the shopping by the ladies was done with my vehicle."

"They were light-hearted people, then? They dined out every evening. Had they a favourite restaurant?"

"Yes, monsieur; most frequently they drove to the Restaurant Rusée in the rue St-Honoré."

"If they come back to this neighbourhood and employ you again, you would find it worth your while to communicate with me. This is my card. Put it in a safe place and don't forget."

"Very good, monsieur."

They ran down the five flights into the street and there Vincent took up the direction of their next move.

"The time has now come," he said, "for an inter-view with Madame Germaine, and in order to save time I suggest that we take a taxi as far as the corner of the rue Duphot. There we will pay off our taxi and proceed on foot to the lady's shop. We will come out into the open and tell her what our mission is. Monsieur Verneuil has already told her about the stolen billhead so she will not be unprepared."

As Goron nodded his agreement, they hailed a taxi and carried out the first part of their plan.

They entered the shop together; Madame Germaine recognized Goron immediately. She smiled diffidently showing a row of beautiful teeth.

"Is Madame already disillusioned with her hat?"

"Not at all: she thinks it charming. But we are come to you on official business. This gentleman is a British colleague from Scotland Yard. I think that Monsieur Verneuil has already seen you about that billhead printed with your name."

"Ah yes! The gentleman called on me this morning. I am shocked that a bill-head of mine should have been stolen and used for criminal purposes."

"Criminal purposes?" queried Vincent with a puzzled expression that he could assume at will.

"Well, when three police officers from two different countries come on the same day to question me, it is natural to assume that it has become a criminal affair."

Vincent registered an inward conviction that if the lady proved to be not all that she pretended she was the finest actress off the stage that he had ever encountered. Nothing seemed to disturb her calm serenity.

"We have called to enquire the addresses of two of your customers, madame," he said. "Two ladies who are American by marriage, but probably not by birth —Madame Blake and Madame Lewis."

"I fear they are no longer in Paris—at any rate they have deserted my shop for some months."

"They were good customers of yours?"

She made a becoming little grimace. "Yes, up to a point they were, but as customers one has to admit that they were exacting, always demanding little alterations in the hats they bought..."

"But they were willing to pay good prices for them?"

"Yes, monsieur, they did not quarrel with the price, and on my side I was careful to be moderate in my charges."

"Will you permit us to enact a little comedy in your shop, madame?" said Goron. "My friend, impersonating you, will go to the window and make believe to take out a hat; I will take the liberty of abstracting one of your bill-heads." He turned to the desk. "Ah, the stage is not properly set for the comedy. There should be a pile of bill-heads lying on this desk."

"They are in the drawer, monsieur, and it is not locked."

"Are they always kept in the drawer?"

"I will not be sure of that, monsieur. It is very possible that on busy days one or two or even more may have been lying on the desk."

"Will you put them as they might have been lying?"

Madame Germaine took out a sheaf of bill-heads and laid them on the desk. Goron, acting as stage manager, signalled to Vincent to go to the window. Then while his companion's back was turned he snatched up a bill-head which he stuffed into his pocket.

"*Eh bien!* my friend. Did you see my felonious act?"

"I saw it perfectly in the mirror on the right."

There was a light laugh from Madame Germaine. "It was a neat little comedy, monsieur. All the properties were in their places and this gentleman was looking in the mirror. Now, if I had been going to the window for a hat I should not have been looking in the mirror; all my attention would have been centred on the hats."

"Madame laughs at the antics of two clumsy men in a hat shop," said Goron. "We must crave pardon for having taken up so much of your time, madame, and take our leave."

When they were out of sight of the shop Goron remarked: "Charming woman, that. Don't you think so?"

"Clever also," agreed Vincent; "and that makes it all the stranger that she should not have seen what was taking place under her nose."

"You mean?"

"I mean that I saw you, in the mirror, abstracting a little book as well as a bill-head."

Goron laughed. "Yes, I have it here, and I propose that we study it together, but I won't swear that she didn't see me take it. Let us go round the corner to the Cafe Veil and look through it together."

It was an ordinary address book, not a commercial ledger. When they had given their order to the waiter, Vincent asked leave to look for an address in the book. He turned to the letter H and pointed triumphantly at Hédouin Belfort. "This name convicts Madame Germaine. They are the great manufacturers and exporters of drugs to the East, but their time is nearly up. The French government is on their track."

"How do you come to know so much about the drug traffic, my friend?" asked Goron.

"Because I happen to be the officer at Scotland Yard who is in charge of the drug question, and in consequence of this I am sent as the British representative to these periodical international meetings in Geneva."

"Not only on account of your special knowledge of the drug question," suggested Goron, "but because of your fluency in our language."

Vincent dismissed the compliment with a gesture and said: "I cannot speak too highly of the behaviour of the French authorities in Syria, which was one of the plague spots of the world in the matter of narcotics. As soon as your government became aware of what was going on they completely destroyed the new crop of hashish which was coming to maturity, and you know that sixty thousand kilograms of hashish a year were being grown in the Lebanon. The Roessler factory of Mulhouse was not the only offender. A certain Dr Hefti had started a flourishing business in Zurich to manufacture dionyl, which was not against the Swiss law, though it is a derivative of hashish."

"I have heard people say that an unnecessary fuss is being made about narcotics; that if the rich choose to indulge in them, no particular harm is done."

"That is the trouble. Let me give you a figure. In Egypt it is estimated that out of a population of fourteen millions, over half a million addicts are to be found, not only among the rich but even among the peasants and labourers. Every village in Egypt, if one may accept the statement of Russell Pasha, who ought to know since he is a chief officer of police, has its heroin addicts and they are the youth of the country. It has been calculated that these are as a rule men between twenty and thirty. Happily so far, the women are free from the vice. But this is only a digression from the business in hand; we have to see whether we can trace any of our friends.

To me, of course, the most important one is Pitt. Let us turn to the P's." He turned the pages and shook his head. "No, the name is not here."

"And yet Germaine's billhead was found on his premises, I believe you said."

"Yes, we found it in the pocket of one of his coats. Then it is evident that Germaine did not deal directly with him, but with an intermediary—probably Blake or Lewis. Let us look for our friend Blake. Why, here he is as large as life, Blake, Hotel Medusa, Cannes. There is no initial: probably it is Madame Blake, acting as a commercial traveller for her husband. Let us see whether Madame Lewis is mentioned?" He fluttered the pages. "Yes, here we are—Lewis, Hotel Medusa, Cannes. They hunt in couples and go to the same nest."

"Good! Then we must pursue them without losing a moment."

"Not so fast, my friend. It's the husbands that I am concerned with—not the wives—and I doubt whether the men could have reached Cannes unless they berthed their boat at the nearest Breton port and took a train southward to the Riviera. How does this idea strike you—to send a telegram addressed, Madame Blake, Hotel Medusa, Cannes. Has monsieur arrived? Reply Poste Restante, rue Cambon, Paris. Germaine?"

Goron nodded his head. "It can do no harm. If you extract a reply that Blake is there you will follow him up, and if there is no reply I suppose that you will turn the matter over to us and return to England? Is it your intention to apply for a warrant of extradiction for murder? It would make our task easier if we had that?"

"That was my idea. If I can leave the question of hunting down these men in your hands, I will go back and obtain the necessary warrant."

The waiter supplied them with a telegraph form and they wrote out their message on the little marble-topped table, paid their account and crossed the boulevard to the rue Cambon.

"While we are waiting for a reply, I suggest that we go to Monsieur Verneuil and tell him what we have done," said Goron.

"Yes. I confess that the ex-petty officer inspires me with confidence. I don't know where he picked up his knowledge of police work, but the French navy was his school for knowledge of human nature. He must have had curious experiences in his career."

"Yes," said Goron dryly, "I've heard some of them. If you want to lose your appetite for dinner, get him to tell you of his adventures in Saigon."

Having sent their telegram, they went on foot to the Exhibition building, along the road that borders the Champs-Élysées as far as the Rond Point. Verneuil received them with a sardonic smile.

"I see that your case is already solved, gentlemen."

"We hope that we are on the way, Monsieur Verneuil; that is, if we may continue to count upon the help you've so freely given us."

Verneuil's eyes narrowed to the merest slit; one might almost say that he winked at the compliment.

"May I assume then," he said in his guttural Southern accent, "that you have come to ask me for further services?"

"It is always better to lay one's cards on the table," said Vincent. "Your conclusion is correct, monsieur: we have come to ask you for further help. The in-formation you gave us about the two Americans Blake and Lewis was valuable. They had two women living with them, presumably their wives; one was seen reading a Russian newspaper; they were passing under the names of Madame Blake and Madame Lewis. Would it be possible for you to trace them?" Verneuil was toying with a pencil and Vincent was glad to notice that it was no longer being employed in drawing diagrams, but was writing.

"You may count upon me to do my best, messieurs. If it were not for the tiresome complication of this attack upon the car of our worthy Socialist leader, I should have more time, but you know what it is with the Paris journals. Some of them love to have a stick with which to belabour the police. I will put your enquiry into competent hands and I suggest that you call upon me again tomorrow."

"Yes, Monsieur Verneuil, but before we go I have something to give you. This little book contains a number of names and addresses."

"Where did you get it?"

"Out of the desk of Madame Germaine of that hat shop."

"You mean she didn't see you take it?"

"I won't be sure of that, monsieur. There is not much that misses the lady's roving eye. But in any case, she must by this time have noticed that the note-book has disappeared. In the meantime we suggest that nothing should be done to alarm her, because she may be acting as a magnet for our two men. But you may care to look through these names and addresses in case they link up with your specialty—the drug traffic. Turn to the page with the letter H, for example, and see whether you recognize a name on that page."

Verneuil ran his eye down the page and stiffened suddenly in his chair. "Hédouin of Belfort. Ah! *par exemple!* Here we have it. The people that I've been trying to trip up for months. We have practically all the evidence that is required, but this woman must be watched."

"Yes," observed Vincent; "when she discovers that her notebook has vanished, she may take to flight."

"If she fancies that she will escape from my observation of her, she will deceive herself. You will leave this book with me, gentlemen? I may find other names."

"Certainly; keep it as long as you think necessary. We do not propose to restore it to the lady."

As they left Verneuil's office Vincent said: "If we go to the rue Cambon on foot would there have been time for a reply to our telegram?"

"It was marked '*Priorité*'; it'll be a near thing: we can but try."

The magic word '*Priorité*' had done the trick; they found a telegram in the Poste Restante also marked '*Priorité*' and addressed to Madame Germaine. Goron asked to see the chief of the telegraph bureau and explained to him that he was in fact, for the moment, Madame Germaine, though the postmaster might find it difficult to believe it. Men charged with the dreary round of postal work are always agog for sensation and here essentially was a case that bristled with drama. Accordingly as soon as he was satisfied about Goron's identity he allowed him to have a copy of the telegram.

The telegram read: "Monsieur still absent abroad. Blake."

"Good," said Goron; "they have fallen into our trap and think that that telegram was sent by Madame Germaine."

"It is possible," said Vincent; "but we must not forget that Germaine is a very clever woman. She may have missed her little book and, assuming that we stole it, may have spent the afternoon calling up her dubious 'customers' on the long-distance telephone, warning them that their addresses are known to the police, who are making inquiries about them."

Chapter Eight

THEY HAD FINISHED dinner; Goron had produced for his guest a bottle of age-old brandy to drink with their coffee. Jacqueline had withdrawn to superintend the woman in the kitchen.

"To return to a question of shop," said Vincent, "there is one point that I should like to study from the map. We will assume for the moment that that telegram was genuine and that Madame Germaine had not put these people on their guard. Have you a map?"

"I have," said Goron, jumping up and laying a motoring map on the table. "You want the coast towns, no doubt."

"Yes," said Vincent. "We may, I think, rule out all ports east of Cherbourg. These men were crossing in a motorboat from Newquay. You will see from the map that there was not much difference between the voyage to Brest or to Cherbourg. In which of these two towns do you think it would be easier for a motorboat whose papers were not quite in order to make a landing without exciting remark?"

"Personally, if I were engaged in any illicit business, I should choose Brest. It is a big town traversed by docks and waterways. An idea strikes me. I have a friend who acts as intelligence officer to the customs at Brest and is well in with all the port officials. If you think of going down I will come with you and introduce you to him."

"That is certainly an idea. As you see, if I stay on in Paris I shall merely be twiddling my thumbs with nothing to do, and when I get home I shall be asked why I stayed so long in France with nothing to show for my expenses. The port offices in Brest must know something of this mysterious boat if she went there and my reason for being in France is to trace that boat and the people who wire in it."

"Then let us have a look at the timetable. There is a morning train...?"

"I must take the night train this evening. It is imperative that I lose no time, but why should I drag you off to the west?"

"Oh, that's all right. I travel free when I'm on duty and this is duty. I am accustomed to night travelling and I can always sleep in the train."

The train they chose left them but a bare hour for preparations. Both men were for quick action at all times, nor was their keenness blunted when they alighted on the Brest platform in the early morning.

In response to a telephone message overnight from Goron, Monsieur Andre Lalage met them on the platform and the introduction was made. Lalage proved to be an alert little man with close-cropped hair standing on end and a huge moustache. He was a Breton born and bred in Brest, who had outshone all his colleagues in the Customs Service by his intelligence and alertness.

"We have much to ask you," said Goron, "and we are trusting to you to find us some *bistro* where we can talk in private."

The little man laughed sardonically. "If you don't mind a *bistro* frequented by dockers, I know of one where we can engage a private room on the first floor."

"Lead on then," said Goron; "we can drink our morning coffee there, I suppose."

"Yes, the coffee is..." he pivoted his hand with fingers outstretched, meaning that he did not answer for the quality of the beverage, "but the bread and the butter are good."

Lalage appeared to be a power at the dockside; the groups of dockers made way for him; one or two of them saluted; he had a kindly word for each.

When the wife of the proprietor of the little café had served them with breakfast and had clumped down the stairs,

Goron made a sign to Vincent to explain his business. There was something about the personality of the Englishman that commended itself. He found his French listeners strongly impressed with his manner of relating the story he had to tell. Even Goron, who had heard it all in Paris, was keenly alive and Lalage could scarcely keep still. He made Vincent repeat the description of the motorboat and nodded his head after each sentence.

"You did well, gentlemen, to come to Brest. It is a port peculiarly adapted to smuggling of all kinds, and as for that motorboat without a name I will tell you how they work. A ship comes in and is examined by the customs officer, who finds the manifest and all the other papers in order. Good! That night a motorboat steals noiselessly up to the seaward side of the ship and throws a parcel or two to the deck hand. Who is to know it, except the deck hand, who of course is in the swim? Some owners employ sworn watchmen, but what is an oath against the flutter of a few notes slipped into his hand on the gangway."

"You mean that the motorboat is owned by somebody in Brest?"

"Yes, there are three or four private motorboats of that kind in the port."

"Without names?"

"Oh, they have a name on their papers, but not always painted on the hulls. A favourite trick is to have alternative names painted on little boards which are hung over the sides and the taffrail."

"The boat we are interested in brought two American passengers to France. Supposing that they landed in Brest, could that be done without the knowledge of the port officers?"

"If it were done at night I think it could. I am speaking to two police officers, so I can speak openly. Money talks and it talks not only to the man who accepts it, but also to his superiors in the Service. That is why I have been busily employed these last few weeks. A customs officer—we will call him 'A'—is living in a house above his means, or he has purchased a car to give his wife a taste of country air on Sundays. The money must come from somewhere and it is my job to follow the scent of it to its source. Generally I succeed, but it entails trying work, I can tell you."

"Then," said Vincent, "if we examine all the motorboats that you have registered in Brest, we shall come upon the craft that we are in search of. The captain speaks English."

Lalage's eyes narrowed. "I know a shorter way than that, monsieur. I have in my service an intelligent young man who made one false step a year ago which merited dismissal. I did not dismiss him; I did not even report the case. I told him that dismissal still hovered above his head like the sword of Damocles, but that as long as he made himself useful to my department the sword would not be permitted to fall."

"He acts then as a spy?"

"Spy is an ugly word, monsieur; we prefer to call him an informant. I can get in touch with him by telephone and in ten minutes he will be here."

The message from the chief of his department had had a nerve-shaking effect upon the informant. Evidently he had feared that another of his sins had found him out. His attitude as he stood in the doorway of that upper room was cringing and his breathing was laboured as if the steep stairs had been too much for him.

"Jules," said Lalage, "you never reported to me that on Sunday last two Americans landed from a motorboat."

"No, monsieur, I did not report it because their papers were all in order and I told them how to get their passports stamped."

"Whose boat did they come in?"

"The *Rosamonde*, Captain Duprez's."

"Is the *Rosamonde* still in the harbour?"

"She is. The captain lives on board always."

"That will do, Jules; if I want you again I'll send for you."

It was with a light-hearted step that Jules descended the stairs from his chief's presence.

"It is possible," said Lalage, "that these two men left the town by train; if they are still in Brest I can find them for you if you will give me the morning for the job. I may even be able to find, if they did leave by train, where they booked to."

"That's very good of you. Meanwhile can we interview the captain of the *Rosamonde*?"

"I was going to suggest that course myself. I will set my men to work and if you will come with me you shall have an interview with the captain. I know where the boat is tied up."

He was as good as his word. In less than a quarter of an hour he returned and conducted them to the quay at which the motorboat was moored.

"There is the *Rosamonde*," he said, pointing to a dark painted motorboat of considerable size. A boy was swabbing down the deck. Lalage hailed him. "Where's your captain?"

"He's gone ashore, monsieur."

"So you're back from England."

The boy looked confused and made no answer.

"Come," said Lalage sternly, "it's no good pretending to be dumb. You were in England on Saturday and you brought back two passengers."

The boy remained silent.

"I can tell you more than that: you anchored in Newquay to pick up those passengers. We know all about it, so it's no good for you to deny it."

"It's not for me to answer; you must ask my captain."

"Where is he?"

"Probably he's in the market. That's where he goes for his provisions."

"How long does he generally take to do his shopping?"

"About half an hour."

"Then we'll come on board and wait for him."

The three police officers had no desire to advertise their presence. They went down into the cabin and Lalage sat down in a position where he could observe the proceedings of the boy. They had not long to wait. Five minutes later the boy converted himself into a human semaphore, pointing significantly to the cabin. On this Goron ran swiftly up on deck and was in time to see a thickset bearded man stop irresolute on the quay and then turn on his heel and walk away with a seaman's rolling gait.

Goron overtook him and tapped him on the shoulder.

"Good morning, Captain."

The man turned savagely upon him. "What do you want with me?"

"A few minutes' conversation. We have taken the liberty of going on board your little vessel to wait for you. Two of my friends are in your cabin at this moment."

For a couple of seconds the man's eyes gleamed.

"Do you want to charter me for a pleasure cruise, or what?"

"I want to discuss business with you."

"Freight?"

"In a sense, yes."

"I don't run freight for anybody that I don't know."

"But you've just been over to England."

"How do you know that? And what else do you know?"

"I know that you picked up a couple of passengers in Newquay on Saturday."

"What if I did? Is it any business of yours?"

"No, but I thought that you might give me an idea of what you charge for a run across the Channel."

"I'll come on board and see your two friends before we talk business."

They returned to the spot where the launch was tied up and jumped on board. At the sight of Lalage, the captain gave a sardonic grin.

"I see that I've been honoured," he said. "I suppose you've searched my little craft from stem to stern, Monsieur Lalage? You look a little downcast so I presume that you found nothing compromising. I'm sorry to have disappointed you."

"I did not come to search your vessel, but only to ask you a question or two about your late passengers. I have their names, of course, but only you can tell me why they chose to come over in your little vessel instead of by one of the ordinary cross Channel boats."

"How can one guess why these eccentric English and Americans choose to cross in a launch; they wanted a new experience, I suppose. But their papers were quite in order."

"Yes, but who told you that they wanted to cross the Channel in this way? Did they write to you, or what?"

"I took them over to England last May, and they enjoyed the voyage so much that they took my address and wrote to me, giving the day for their return passage."

"When you were at Newquay," put in Vincent, "you had no name on your boat. Why was that?"

The captain laughed. "I see that you know very little about the vagaries of holiday makers. If they have ladies with them

it is a game among them to name the boat. Look, monsieur."
He opened a locker and showed little boards with names
painted on them. "If a majority of the ladies is in favour of
Rosamonde then I hang out these boards and the boat be-
comes *Rosamonde* as she is registered, but if they prefer the
name of Iris, well, here are the little boards to hang out."

Lalage became stern. "Your boat is registered as
Rosamonde and you change the name at your own risk. The
whims of lady passengers do not count in a matter like this.
See to it that the name *Rosamonde* is painted on the boat or
there may be trouble in store for you."

"Very good, monsieur," replied the captain in a surly tone.

Vincent interposed with another question. "Where is the
letter you received from these Americans asking you to meet
them at Newquay?"

"I never keep letters; they go overboard when I've read
them."

"What address did they give at the head of the letter?"

"None that I remember."

"And, of course," suggested Lalage sarcastically, "you
don't remember the name of the hotel they went to in Brest."

"I never knew where they went to. They just took their
handbags and walked off."

"Well," said Lalage, rising, "don't forget my order about
the name of this boat: that it is to be painted on her and not
on boards to be hung over the side; and see to it that you
don't accept charters for passengers whose papers are not
in order." He lowered his voice. "Remember that you will be
held responsible for any prohibited article imported by any
of your passengers. Take this warning to heart because if you
neglect it and you are prosecuted, it will be brought to the
knowledge of the magistrate."

When they were on shore again, Lalage remarked: "I never expected to get any admission from that rascal. Clearly, he has been squared by the gang, but this interview may make him think twice before he accepts those Americans as passengers again..." A telegraph boy was approaching. He was scrutinizing the names on the small craft as he went. Lalage stopped him.

"Who's your telegram for?"

"Captain Duprez, of the *Rosamonde*."

"I've just come from the *Rosamonde*. You know me, my lad. I will take charge of this telegram."

"Yes, I know you, monsieur, but..."

"That's all right. You can tell the postmaster that I took charge of it."

The boy handed over the telegram and required Lalage to sign a receipt for it. He went off whistling some kind of tune. As soon as he had turned the corner Lalage tore the confining strip of blue paper and read aloud:

"BRING BOAT TO ST MALO. URGENT."

"Good!" exclaimed Vincent. "We'll go to St Malo. What's the quickest way?"

"If you come to my office the timetable will tell you. I don't carry all the cross-country trains in my head. We will also see whether my men, who have been out tracing these men, have brought in any report."

They found a man in plain clothes waiting in the office.

"Any news, Henri?"

"Yes, monsieur, those two Americans were staying at the Hotel des Cloches and left early this morning —in haste. Fortunately their room had not been touched since their departure and in the empty fireplace we found this." He brought out a piece of blue paper screwed into a tight ball.

Lalage smoothed it out. "*Tiens!* Yet another telegram. Ah! You must read this, monsieur: it is in English." He handed it to Vincent.

Vincent interpreted the telegram into French. It ran:

CAUTION. SCENT IS STRONG. GERMAINE.

"Ah! Madame Germaine assured us that she understood not a word of English, yet she writes her telegram in that language."

Chapter Nine

"IF I MIGHT make a suggestion," said Vincent, "I think that the best route for us to St Malo would be by motorboat—the boat of Captain Duprez."

Goron threw up his arms and brought his palms heavily down upon his knees. "You've hit it, my friend. The sea is calm and during our little voyage there would be time for conversation. Who knows but that our sturdy sea captain may experience a change of heart in the course of the voyage. We could leave it to our English friend here to apply the necessary mental treatment."

"Do you suggest that I should give him the telegram?" asked Lalage.

"On no account," exclaimed Vincent. "If he had that telegram, he would not take us. But which of us is going to charter the boat?"

"I think that Monsieur Lalage is the obvious person," said Goron. "There is no time to lose. Will you go back alone and make the necessary overtures?"

"I will," said Lalage, "and I'll apply pressure if necessary. Give me ten minutes and then you can come along to the boat to hear what is decided. If all goes well I will make an unobtrusive signal to you by lifting my hand to my face and rubbing my right eyebrow."

In ten minutes by Vincent's watch the two police officers sauntered along the quay towards the launch. When they came in sight of the *Rosamonde*, Goron murmured: "Keep your eye on Lalage."

Almost as he spoke both saw Lalage bring his right hand to his eye and begin a vigorous rubbing of his eyebrow.

"Good!" said Vincent; "we're over the first fence."

"The second offence will be your affair; I am curious to see how you will set about it."

The first part of their voyage was quite uneventful. They stopped to take in motor fuel and then continued on their way along the coast towards St Malo.

Vincent was regarding the captain with a fixed stare. The man had his hand on the tiller and it was obvious that the scrutiny disconcerted him.

"You seem to be uneasy, my friend. You think that I am looking at you more closely than is consistent with good manners. You must excuse me. I was speculating how you would look in the striped overall that they wear at Cayenne."

The man stifled an oath and the boat lurched dangerously towards the rock-bound shore. Vincent made a leap towards the tiller and seized it firmly, bringing the head of the launch parallel to the coast.

"Your steering is erratic, my friend. Let me remind you that we are bound for St Malo, not for the next world. You had better leave the steering to me."

The Breton captain still kept his hand on the tiller for the sake of appearances, but he allowed Vincent to control the steering.

"I am always sorry when I see a man backing the wrong horse at the races, and it grieves me when I think of a man accustomed to the wild fresh air and liberty of the seas heading towards a narrow little cubicle in a cell of corrugated iron, deprived of such amenities as tobacco. They tell me that that deprivation is the worst part of imprisonment; that men would sell their souls for a twist of tobacco leaf. The pity of it is that if you were working for the lawful authorities you would have a quiet life and an easy conscience."

"I don't know what you're talking about. I'm a plain sailor."

"Then let us talk in plain language as man to man," retorted Vincent. "You have been carrying passengers from England with dangerous contraband about their persons."

"I know nothing about that. People take their passage and that's all that concerns me."

"Then why not prove your innocence by helping the police to do their duty?"

"What do you want me to do?"

"I'll tell you. We hold a telegram sent to you by those two men, telling you to come to St Malo for them. They are expecting you. What we want you to do when you catch sight of them on the quay is to signal that all is well. Probably you have a code of signals."

"You are an Englishman. You couldn't arrest me."

"I might have to denounce you to the French authorities and they have a short way with their nationals who engage in the drug traffic. You might find yourself languishing in a prison cell for months before being brought to trial and all that time you would be on a prison diet, with nothing to smoke and aid digestion. Why, man! Your health would break down under the strain."

"Do those gentlemen in the cabin, who are French officers, want me to do this?"

"They do and they will tell you so." He signalled to Goron and Lalage to come out of the cabin. The captain now proved to be amenable and their plans were made.

As they neared the quay at St Malo, Vincent's heart beat fast when he saw two men waving. They answered the description of those of whom he was in search. It was possible that they were armed and would resist capture, but that was a risk that every police officer had to take. He was relieved to see that there were other people on the quay. The presence of so many witnesses might restrain the two criminals from using their revolvers.

The three officers remained out of sight in the cabin as the captain steered his launch to the steps. The two men advanced confidently and Vincent leaped for the lowest of the granite steps, followed by Goron and Lalage. The men had not a chance to make off.

Goron laid his hand on the shoulder of the nearest saying: "You are wanted at the police station."

"What for?"

"They will tell you that at the station."

"I demand first to be taken to the American consulate," said the man. "You have no right to interfere with American citizens."

"You are now on French soil, monsieur, and you may both have to answer charges of breaking French law, but you shall have an opportunity of telephoning to the American consulate from the police station."

"What is the charge? We have a right to know that."

Vincent caught a quick glance in the eyes of one of the men towards one of the little streets that debouched upon the quay. He was measuring his chance of escape. It was the moment for a word of warning in English. "You had better not try to do a bolt," Vincent said. "They have a short way over here with prisoners who resist arrest. I advise you to go quietly."

"You hear that?" shouted the man to his companion. "This guy is a cop from Scotland Yard. These Britishers won't let the French do their own dirty work without interfering. O.K., we'll go with you, but you'll get hell from the State Department in Washington when they get to hear of it, I warn you."

Vincent interposed quietly. "There are charges pending against you in England and there may be extradition proceedings. I can tell you no more than that at this stage."

The men now appeared to accept the inevitable and followed Lalage without another word. Vincent did some rapid thinking. He drew Goron out of earshot.

"I shall have to get into communication with my chief at Scotland Yard."

"By telephone, you mean?"

"No, I think it best that I should return to England if you can assure me that the men will be held safely in custody here until their extradition is arranged."

"Have no fear," responded Goron. "You can safely leave them with us."

"Then I will lose no more time. I must make enquiries about the boats."

"I must accompany M. Lalage and these men. If you don't get a boat for this evening come round to the little *bistro* and we'll meet again there."

"I will. In case we don't meet again, please accept my warmest thanks for your help."

He shook hands with both his French colleagues and made his way to the steamship office. He was just in time to get a passage on a boat that was leaving within an hour.

On his way back to England Vincent reflected a little ruefully on the difficulties that lay before him in persuading the powers above that this was a case in which extradition might properly be applied for. He knew that it would be useless to cite the drug traffic because this was not at that period one of the scheduled offences to which extradition applied, even if the evidence had been sufficient to convince the Director of Public Prosecutions that it was a water-tight case. That is always the difficulty that confronts police officers. They may be certain that an offender is breaking the law, but unless they have evidence sufficient to convince a court of justice their hands are tied. The wide powers conferred on the police under the Defence of the Realm Act had been repealed for more than ten years. They were now back in the old rut in which personal liberty even of the criminal counted for more than the safety of the public.

True, there was the question of the murder charge, but a charge of wilful murder is not lightly to be preferred on evidence that was largely circumstantial and even more largely conjectural.

On arriving in London, Vincent reported himself to his immediate superior, Chief Constable Richardson, who listened patiently to his story and said that the proper course was to go over to the Director of Public Prosecutions to lay the whole case before him. This was an ordeal that in former days had daunted most men in the department, for there came a moment when the director put his elbows on the table and joined the fingertips of both hands before he spoke. His speech on those occasions damped the spirits of most of his colleagues, for the gesture was invariably followed by destructive criticism. Vincent's hope was that he would find the assistant director in temporary charge of the department: he could always deal with that gentleman.

It was not to be. The director himself was in his room and disengaged. He was a curious product of the departmental machine. His name had been prominent in the newspaper reports of most of the important criminal cases as prosecutor for the Crown; his appointment as Director of Public Prosecutions had therefore occasioned no surprise and very little heartburning from those of his profession who aspired to the appointment. He had been knighted; he was now a permanent official like any other civil servant but he had retained the forensic mannerisms of his earlier days at the Bar, being neither fish nor fowl, since he had not been through the Civil Service mill that grinds all men to something of the same pattern. Sir John Manning wore a fringe of grey hair about the conical dome of his skull; otherwise his skin was naked, not, it was alleged by the subordinate members of his staff, through the attentions of the razor, but because Nature, in designing him, had taken the hen's egg for the model to work upon and had denied him the hirsute adornments that decorated his fellow men. But lest anyone should think that there was anything feminine in his make-up, she had endowed him with the deepest of bass voices, at which timid solicitors' clerks introduced without warning into the Presence had been known to leap three inches from their chairs.

It was not the first time that Vincent had been required to undergo the ordeal, indeed he found that he was a *persona grata* with the great man.

"Well, Mr Vincent, what are you bringing us to-day?—something interesting, I feel sure. Someone told me that you had gone abroad on a confidential mission."

"Yes, Sir John, and I am just back."

"Did your travels take you as far as Geneva? I was there the other day and I was immensely struck with that great building they have erected for the League of Nations. You have seen it, of course?"

"Yes, Sir John, and I have attended little international conferences in one of the rooms there."

"On criminal questions, I suppose?"

"Yes, Sir John. On the drug traffic and on the question of the form of cheque which would be proof against forgery. The interest lay in the fact that even the Americans had deputed their expert police officers to attend."

"I am glad to think that the League of Nations is serving *some* useful purpose; otherwise there will be nothing for it but to convert that building into a hospital for incurables."

"I am not sure, Sir John, that it has not already gone some way in that direction, judging from the curious long-haired people that one meets in the corridors."

"But we are gossiping about international politics when we ought to be talking business. You have something to tell me."

Thereupon Vincent gave him a succinct account of the problem that was facing him. When he had finished, the fingertips of the director came together. "If I understand you correctly you suggest that there are grounds for applying for extradition on the charge of wilful murder. Is that correct?"

"Yes sir, it is."

"The evidence, as I see it, is purely circumstantial —the hiring of a car, the breaking of one of the windows by a revolver bullet, the finding of the body of a murdered man by a witness who can be produced, and this coat that was found in the tool box of the hired car. I confess that I have known stronger cases; but when I have your report I will go very carefully through it and send for you again. In the meantime I understand that the men in question are being safely held by the French authorities."

"That is so, sir. Thank you very much. I will go and write my report at once."

On his way to the chief inspector's room Vincent knocked at his chief constable's door and was at once admitted.

"Well," said his chief, "what did the director say?"

"He told me to go and write my report, sir, and he would consider whether there were sufficient grounds for charging these men with murder. In that case he did not anticipate any difficulty in obtaining an extradition warrant."

"Very well," said Richardson, "you had better lose no time in writing your report, but let me see it first."

To Vincent, writing a convincing report was child's play. He was a strict economist in words, but that was so refreshing a contrast with the reports of many of his colleagues that he had no fear about the verdict of the director, nor did his chief constable find any fault with it.

"Right. You can take that round to the director and tell him, if you like, that I have seen it."

All this had eaten away the morning and Vincent was beginning to feel the pangs of hunger. He was about to make his way up to the floor where dinners were served when a telegram was put into his hands. He tore open the envelope and felt on reading the message that all appetite for food had deserted him. The message was signed "Goron." It was quite brief.

BOTH MEN ESCAPED FROM CUSTODY DURING
THE NIGHT.

There was nothing for it but for Vincent to take the telegram to his chief and ask for further instructions. For once, Richardson betrayed impatience. "Thank God," he said, "that our men know how to hold their prisoners without giving all this trouble. You'll have to run over to France again."

"To Paris, sir?"

"Yes, because by this time Goron must have returned to duty in Paris and rascals of this kind would find Paris their safest hiding place."

"Very good, sir; I'll cross by the night boat to Dieppe—unless you think that it would be better to take St Malo on the way?"

"No. You must go to Paris. Get into touch with M. Verneuil again, as well. He is not very quick in the uptake but when the scent is strong he never abandons the chase."

Chapter Ten

ON ARRIVING at the Gare St Lazare, Vincent's first objective was the Ministry of the Interior. He went straight to Goron's room and was fortunate enough to find him alone.

"Come in, my friend. I am very glad to see you. I thought it not improbable that my telegram might bring you again to Paris, where you are always welcome."

"Thank you. The atmosphere of Paris is always exhilarating to the jaded Londoner but, on this occasion, it has been your bad news that has brought me. Those rascals have escaped?"

"Yes. I can scarcely contain myself when I think of the laxity of these provincial police officers, if indeed it was slackness and not bribery."

"I should not have dared to make that suggestion myself, but since you have made it...One must remember that the profits in the drug traffic are so considerable that bribes can be offered on quite a liberal scale. M. Verneuil may have found some corroborative evidence in Madame Germaine's address book showing that our surmise that drugs are concerned in this case was correct."

"Then let us go and see M. Verneuil."

By this time they had become familiar figures to the door-keeper, who saluted them with a forefinger and indicated the lift. Verneuil received them with his usual bluff welcome and inquired after their health. As usual, in the public offices in France, minutes were expended in the preliminary courtesies.

"Pleased as I am to see you, my friend," said Verneuil, "I feel sure that it is the laxity of those miserable police in St Malo in allowing those rascals to escape that has brought you back to France."

"It is," put in Goron, "but I have assured our English colleague that they should be recaptured if they are still on French soil. Orders have been given to all ports and frontier towns to stop them. And now, to turn to another phase of the case, did you find that little book of any use to you?"

"Yes. The most important bit of evidence it contains is the name of that suspected factory in Belfort. As you were averse from alarming the lady by direct interview, I put her premises under observation and my man is instructed to make notes of every visitor to the shop. He is one of my most trusted officers, so you need have no misgivings."

He had scarcely finished speaking when there was a tap on the door and a young man with deep anxiety graven on his features exposed his head to view and at once withdrew it on seeing that his chief was not alone.

"Ah, this is the man I posted to watch those premises. Come in, André," he shouted. "What have you to report?"

"Monsieur, in some mysterious way, that woman in the rue Duphot has disappeared. Yesterday afternoon and this morning a number of people came and tried the door of her shop. Some of the more impatient thumped on the door. This morning the baker called with bread but could get no one to take it in."

"But there are no back entrances to those old shops in the rue Duphot."

"That is true, monsieur."

"And yet you are satisfied that she did not leave by the front door?"

"Quite satisfied, monsieur."

A flush began to suffuse Verneuil's weather-beaten countenance as a horrible suspicion assailed him.

"Did no vehicle stop at the shop door while you were on duty?"

"No, monsieur, except of course the baker this morning, who tried the door and went away."

"And yesterday?"

"Only the laundry van, late in the afternoon."

"And the driver carried into the shop an empty basket—a basket large enough for a week's family washing?"

"Yes, monsieur, it was a large basket: it required the driver and another man to carry it."

"And after a few minutes they came out again with the basket and loaded it into the van?"

"Yes, monsieur," replied the watcher, surprised at the intuition of his questioner.

"My God! That any Parisian should be so lacking in intelligence as to let that basket pass unopened."

"Why, monsieur? It was an ordinary laundry basket."

"And I suppose that you would describe yourself as a man of ordinary intelligence? But if you had raised the lid of that basket you would have had the shock of your life. It had a woman in it."

The poor constable looked as if this last remark was all the shock he needed.

"Well, you will say that you were only told to watch for people who came and went on their two legs—not for ladies who chose to be carried out in laundry baskets. But there it is. The harm is done. Can you give me a description of the people who tried the door after the laundry van had gone?"

"Well, monsieur, now I come to think of it, I remember only one; a tall, thin man, with a face like a hatchet."

"Come, you can give me a better description of him than that. What age was he?"

"Between thirty and forty, I should say. He was dressed like an Englishman."

"You mean that he went to a good tailor for his clothes?"

"Yes, monsieur, the clothes were certainly not sold to him ready made."

"Thank you, André. I shall want nothing more for the present," said Verneuil.

The man's air was crestfallen as he went out: he knew that there would be more to come about his lack of intuition.

"*Mon Dieu!*" said Verneuil. "We seem not to be distinguishing ourselves in this affair, but it may not be so difficult to find the lady as you suspect. We have first to trace that laundry van."

"Her uneasiness is not difficult to explain," said Vincent. "She must have missed that little book of hers and the man on observation was not concealing the fact that he was posted to watch her. She thought an unobtrusive disappearance was the safest card to play. Now I'm wondering if the tall, thin man who called at the shop could have been Lewis."

"Would he be such a fool," said Goron, "as to run his head into the lion's mouth by calling at the shop?"

"Well, Germaine had warned the wives, but the women could not pass on the warning to the men, as apparently they were not in touch with them."

"Listen," said Verneuil. "I mean to get to the bottom of this escape from St Malo. In this little book," he fluttered the pages of Madame Germaine's notebook, "there is an address P.H., 9, rue de la Couronne, St Malo. Who can P.H. be?"

"Why not telephone to the St Malo police?" suggested Vincent.

"I was on the point of doing so when you gentlemen came in."

The telephoning did not take long. Within ten minutes they were in possession of the fact that the address was that of the mayor himself, Philippe Henriques.

"Things are beginning to warm up," murmured Goron. "In a port such as St Malo the mayor has opportunities—very profitable opportunities—and if those two criminals could get into friendly touch with him we need be surprised at nothing."

"Well," said Vincent, "assuming that money has passed and that the major was at the bottom of the escape, what is to be our next step? My only concern in this matter is to get hold of those two men and see that they are safely held in custody in France, leaving me free to go over to London and get extradition warrants signed. As I had to return on receipt of your telegram there was no time to get them."

"You can rest assured," said Verneuil grimly, "that the next time they are caught, they will not escape."

"If one of them, as we believe, called on Madame Germaine as late as yesterday evening, probably both the men are in Paris at this moment. It seems to me that the obvious step is to call upon that concierge in their old lodgings and the driver of the taxi which they were in the habit of using."

"I could get these enquiries done at once in the arrondissement, but I don't think that we had better spread this business too widely," said Verneuil.

"My main interest," said Goron, "is in the drug traffic now that the connection of these men with drugs is established.

You, my friend, are concerned only with getting these men arrested on charges of murder. Is that not so?"

"I feel that we are all sailing in the same boat, gentlemen," said Vincent, "for we are all concerned—deeply concerned—in the arrest of these two rascals, Blake and Lewis."

"I think we may safely leave the enquiries in Paris to our friend here, who, when once he undertakes a delicate enquiry, never lets go until he gets what he wants," said Goron.

Verneuil acknowledged the compliment with a curl of the lip, intended to indicate that he did not accept compliments at their face value. He knew his own value—none better—and he knew where he was likely to fail in enquiries that required the delicate touch of a trained diplomatist, but he could well imagine what a mess most trained diplomatists would make of police enquiries. In private conversation he was apt to describe the Foreign Office clerks as "those young ladies."

"Well, Vincent," continued Goron, "I think that you and I will take one of the official cars to St Malo and engage in a friendly conversation with his Worship the Mayor. I suggest that messages should be sent to the port officers and the officers on all frontiers to exercise very special vigilance. I will get that done. If you'll come with me to the Ministry of the Interior we'll commandeer our car and start as soon as possible."

When the other two had gone, Verneuil resolved to leave nothing to subordinates. He would undertake the business singlehanded. His enquiries at the lodgings and of the taxi driver met with no result. Neither the concierge nor the chauffeur had seen either the men or their wives since February. Verneuil knew how to extract the truth from people like this and was satisfied that they were not lying. His next visit was to the rue Duphot. He was well provided with all that was needed for dealing with locked doors. In this case the door was furnished with a Yale lock that snapped to. But what Verneuil did not know about Yale locks and the manner of bringing them to a friendly understanding was not worth knowing.

He was going to make a thorough search of the premises, but he turned first to the letter box. Empty? No. One letter. And there was no need to steam it open, for the addressee would never come to know of the outrage to her correspondence perpetrated with the grimy thumb of an ex-petty officer.

The letter was quite short and would have puzzled any unauthorized reader who did not know the facts with which Verneuil was acquainted. It was signed "P. H." and it read as follows:

> ...the carrier pigeons have been released and if their instinct guides them aright you may find them roosting on your window ledge even before you receive this letter. They will need food and drink and a little kindness from you.

Verneuil's comment was terse. "'Pigeons,' he calls them! Why stop at 'pigeons' when he might have said 'doves'? Oh, these provincial mayors, they make me tired."

Would there be time to catch Goron and Vincent before their departure for the north? He did not stop to search the rest of the premises but hailed a taxi, directing the driver to the Ministry of the Interior.

He was in time; a car was taking in petrol in the courtyard of the Ministry when his taxi drew up.

Goron was about to take his seat when Vincent touched him on the arm.

"Here comes Verneuil. I think he wants us."

The ex-petty officer, a little out of breath, came hurrying up.

"I have brought you this letter, gentlemen. You may find it useful when interviewing his Worship the Mayor."

"Where did you get it?"

"Out of Madame Germaine's letter box. She was not there to receive her own correspondence; that is the obvious objection to leaving home in a laundry basket. Good hunting!" said Verneuil. "I need not detain you longer. I have my work cut out in tracing the laundry man who received Madame Germaine in his basket."

He turned on his heel and was gone.

The journey to St Malo was uneventful. They arrived at the chief police office at half-past four, for Goron had a bone to pick with the police officers. He made himself known to the inspector in charge as Commissaire Goron of the Sûreté Nationale.

As when a sudden gust of wind stirs the growing corn the announcement of his rank produced consternation among the men in the police office. He asked to see the principal Commissaire, who made his appearance unshaven, in an unbuttoned tunic. There was a hunted look in his eyes, the look that a man wears when his sins have found him out.

"So the men that I handed over to you, monsieur, for safe custody contrived to escape? In order that I may be in a position to make my report to the Minister, I should like to be shown the cell from which the escape was made and hear your explanation of how it occurred."

"Very good, monsieur; if you will give yourself the trouble of following me, I will take you down to the cells."

The door was unlocked and a recalcitrant Norwegian sailor, who had been sampling French wines too lavishly, was removed into the corridor while Goron inspected the window bars. He could find nothing wrong with them. He turned upon the police officer and demanded how he explained the escape. "Those window bars were intact?"

"Yes, monsieur, I am even now enquiring from my staff how the escape could have been contrived."

"I think I can tell you," said Goron dryly, "how it was contrived and who contrived it, but let that pass. Tell me, M. le Commissaire, did the mayor visit the prisoners on the evening of their arrest?"

"He did, monsieur. You had said that they might telephone to the American Consul, so naturally I allowed them to telephone also to the mayor when they asked."

Goron drew Vincent a little aside and said: "You see, I was not far wrong. These men hold their appointment from the mayor. It would serve no good purpose for us to drag out the details of this discreditable proceeding. It is the mayor whom we want."

Chapter Eleven

THE MAYOR LIVED in a flat on the second floor, filled with a heterogeneous mass of second-hand furniture of various ages and styles picked up at sales. In private life he was an advocate, though his practice in a place like St Malo could not have been remunerative. It was obvious that he depended on other sources for his income. All this Vincent and Goron took in at a glance while they were waiting for the mayor to make his appearance.

When he did appear he was obviously nervous and ill at ease. Goron's card was sufficient to account for this, for any communication from the Ministry of the Interior always sent cold shivers down his spine and this card indicated that Goron was a police functionary.

The two police officers rose. Goron made the necessary introduction of Vincent and the mayor's frightened eyes took on a new aspect of alarm. It was not only the Ministry of the Interior which was concerned with his doings, but an official from the famous institution on the banks of the Thames. Clearly, trouble was brewing.

"We have taken the liberty of calling on you, Monsieur le Maire," said Goron, "in connection with the escape of two prisoners from the cells in the police station."

"Yes, monsieur; it was a most lamentable occurrence."

"So lamentable, that the minister of the interior will want to know from me exactly how it happened. I am told that you had an interview with these two men while they were in the cells. May I go so far as to inquire what was the object of this interview?"

The mayor gulped and swallowed. It gave him time to prepare the answer to this embarrassing question. "I was doing my bare duty, monsieur; the police of the municipality being under my control, I felt that I should be failing in my duty if I did not satisfy myself that the prisoners were being properly treated."

"That I quite understand," said Goron. "The two men were, I presume, confined in the same cell. They did not escape through the window."

The mayor was about to reply when Goron held up his hand to stop the interruption. "That I know from personal enquiry at the police station. They escaped through the door, but the door was not damaged in any way and the locks and bolts were intact; therefore it was obvious that they escaped through collusion with one or other of your police. May I ask what you are doing about this?"

"I am going to hold a very searching enquiry," replied the mayor, "and if I find that any of my officers were responsible for the escape, he will be severely dealt with. Of that you may be sure."

"I am pushing my enquiry a little further than I should have done were it not for a letter signed 'P.H.' found by the Paris police in the letter box of a lady whose conduct, I fear, leaves something to be desired. It occurred to me right to show this letter to you, since it bears your initials, and ask you whether it was typed on your machine?"

The mayor took the letter with trembling fingers and made as if to read it. Vincent watched him narrowly the while and satisfied himself that his eyes were not following the lines and that his mind was engaged in speculating about the reply that would be most likely to find acceptance.

"It is most unlikely, monsieur, that anyone should have had access to my machine. It is used occasionally by my clerk, but she could not have written a letter of this kind. For one thing, I have no carrier pigeons, nor have the police."

It had gradually been borne in upon Vincent that, so far from being a leader or the brains of the gang, the mayor was a mere cog in the machine; Goron, on the other hand, was thinking of the report that he would make to his chiefs in the Ministry of the Interior on the subject of the mayor and of the policemen under him. He intended to call attention to the deplorable effect it would have in London on the reputation of the French authorities: that, he knew, would set many wheels revolving.

"I don't think we need trouble you further, Monsieur le Maire," said Goron. "I have sufficient material for my report to the minister. I will only trouble you further in asking you to let me use your typewriter for a moment. My case will then be complete."

The mayor stammered an inarticulate reply, but Goron maintained his bland attitude. "You will not refuse to allow me to use your machine?"

It was useless to attempt concealment, for the machine was standing in full view in a corner of the room. Goron swept off the cover and proceeded to type with unexpected agility a copy of the letter signed "P.H." found in the Germaine hat shop in the rue Duphot.

He compared the two, noting all the defects in the typescript of both and marking them with a blue pencil.

"Look, Monsieur le Maire," he said, as if he had just made a discovery, "this is indeed a curious co-incidence, for if you compare these two copies you might be tempted to say that they had been written on the same machine, and yet you think that most unlikely. But in Paris they have typewriting experts...if ever it came to an official investigation...especially since your address appears in such questionable company in a list recently acquired by the Paris police—that, you know," added Goron pleasantly, "is how we knew where to find 'P.H.'"

The poor mayor was not made of cast steel. The Day of Judgment had come upon him without any preparation. The power of speech had abandoned him; he could only bleat inarticulately.

"You wish to tell us something confidentially, I think, Monsieur le Maire?" said Goron.

"Yes, monsieur. There is much to tell, and if I have a solemn promise from you two gentlemen that I shall be exempt from prosecution and that nothing that I say will be disclosed to any journalist, I will tell you everything that I know."

Goron seemed to waver about giving this undertaking, but Vincent intervened. "No hint will be given by us to the journalists, Monsieur le Maire. If they learn anything it will be through the indiscretion of a member of your own staff. As to the question of prosecution…"

"We are not in a position to give any pledge, but if you come forward as a witness for the Procureur Général I suppose that the usual course will be followed," said Goron.

The mayor hesitated. He appeared to be putting a strain upon what he would have described as his brain. But once he had got under way, the information which he vouchsafed was of absorbing interest to Vincent. To begin with, he admitted quite frankly that he was in league with drug traffickers and that Madame Germaine, in Paris, was mixed up with those chartered to distribute the poison. A few tactful questions brought out further admissions. His special duty was to keep watch on the ports of the northern coast through colleagues who were concerned to some extent in the same traffic, and to give facilities to boats entering or leaving. Moreover, he had agreed to be at the disposal of foreign drug runners—such as Blake and Lewis, whose names were well known to him.

Goron had taken charge of the questions up to this point, but now Vincent broke in. "When these men escaped, where did they go?"

The mayor hesitated. "I do not know."

"Think again, Monsieur le Maire. You knew that they were going to Paris because you wrote to Madame Germaine to warn her. Is that not so?"

The mayor inclined his head. He seemed to be beyond articulate speech.

"Very well. If you know so much, you must also know where they stay in Paris."

This was a question that the mayor could answer truthfully. "I assure you, gentlemen, that I do not know that. All that

I had to do was to pass the word to Madame Germaine. She would surely know that."

Vincent now left his French colleague to take up the interrogation again.

"You could not be doing all this unless you had some influential person in Paris to cover you in case of trouble."

"You are perfectly right, monsieur; I am told that there is no less a person than a deputy who will protect us when things go wrong."

"His name?"

"That I cannot tell you. I have never heard his name."

"At present I shall not insist; but it will have to come out. He is your protector."

"Yes, monsieur, he is more than merely our protector; he gives us advice."

"You mean advice for nothing?"

"Oh no, monsieur. The advice, I believe, is very expensive, but that does not concern me. The gentleman has access to ministers; he is a person that counts in the political world; occasionally he visits the prime minister, if not the President of the Republic."

"And who provides the money for oiling his palm?"

"I understand that it comes from America, but in such a form that it cannot be traced."

"Who brings it?"

"These men Blake and Lewis were expected to bring quite a formidable sum."

"Apart from this important person whose name you do not know, who would you say is the centre of the organization?"

"Perhaps Madame Germaine—I do not know. I assure you, gentlemen, that I am not told names; I receive orders to carry out from time to time and when these two men telephoned to me from the prison cells, I knew that my duty was to let them escape, and they dictated the message to Madame Germaine. I thought, of course, that the deputy in question would protect me."

Vincent consulted Goron with his eyes, and noting that his colleague made an answering signal, he rose from his seat to indicate that he had no further questions to ask. "I must lose no time in communicating with my chief in London, M. Goron. You will guide me to the office of the long-distance telephone?"

"I do earnestly hope," said the mayor, addressing his remarks to Goron, "that I shall not be implicated in any action you may take? I hope that you will allow it to appear that your action is taken in consequence of information that has reached the Sûreté, giving no names and especially guarding against embroiling me with any minister or deputy."

"You will understand, Monsieur le Maire, that my action in this interview has been entirely guided by a sense of duty; that I have no kind of animosity towards you and that you may count upon me to keep your name out of the business as far as possible. We will now take our leave of you."

As they went down the stairs Vincent observed: "You were very polite and friendly towards the mayor, considering the part he has played in this business."

"One never knows what one of these mayors may some day become in the country. I might encounter him as minister of the interior and my chief."

"It is easy to see why they do not trust so stupid a man with names. He would blurt them out and ruin the whole organization on the slightest hint of trouble to himself."

"We shall have to use a broom and sweep out all the doubtful characters in these northern ports. What would I not give for the name of that deputy, but it's obvious that the mayor was not entrusted with it."

Chapter Twelve

IT TOOK an unconscionable time to get connected with Chief Constable Richardson at New Scotland Yard. Apparently half the population of France was eager to telephone to half the population of Great Britain, for, according to the operator, the line remained occupied and there were others before Vincent waiting for their turn. At last Vincent heard the voice he knew. He gave a succinct account of what he had done and asked for instructions whether he should go to Paris to pursue his enquiries or leave the French police to carry on. The reply was emphatic.

"Now that you've gone so far, it would be foolish to throw up the sponge. You must go to Paris and I will cover your expenses with the Receiver."

Goron was waiting outside the telephone booth.

"It's all right," said Vincent. "We are to travel to Paris together."

Goron's face beamed. "I don't know how it is, my friend, but I must confess that I should feel entirely lost without you. You may not have the same feeling as regards myself, but I confess that I find you more like a brother than a colleague."

"I, too, have the same feeling for you, my friend," replied Vincent, "and I think that we shall always have the same kind of feeling for one another. We had better see that our car is filled up with petrol and get on our way. An interview with our friend Verneuil is necessary."

Both were busy with their own thoughts on the journey to Paris; they exchanged scarcely a syllable. At the commissariat of police they met Verneuil coming down the stairs, thinking that he had finished work for the day, but on recognizing his visitors he insisted on taking them up to his office.

"But you were just going out."

"Only to consume an *apéritif* at the Rond Point—a bad habit into which one so easily falls. Besides, I have some news that may interest you. We have located the laundry in whose basket we believe Madame Germaine escaped."

"Have you done anything about it?" asked Vincent, rather eagerly.

"Not yet, monsieur, beyond putting that laundry under observation. The fact is, I was keeping any further steps until your return to Paris. Needless to say I am having every basket that passes in or out examined by one of my officers."

"Is the laundry doing any genuine business?" asked Vincent.

"Oh yes, its van goes round collecting work from the best residents in the quarter. It has a considerable staff of laundry women and the proprietor lives with his wife in a flat above the laundry itself. I have made enquiries of the concierge and have ascertained that no strange lady is staying with the proprietor and his wife."

"I suppose we could visit the working part of the laundry?"

"Certainly, if I go with you, but at this hour of the day the workpeople have gone home and the place is locked up."

"I should like to see these workpeople arrive in the morning," said Vincent.

"You think that Madame Germaine may have converted herself into a laundry woman?" asked Goron.

"I think that possible; at any rate it would be easier to make a recognition when women are dressed for the street than when they are in working kit."

"You are quite right, my friend. The working kit of a woman is a good disguise."

"It will mean an early start," said Verneuil. "You will have to meet me here not later than eight if we are to see them all come in."

"Eight o'clock sharp then," said Vincent after consulting Goron. "And now, my friends, I have a proposition to make. It is that we find a quiet restaurant to dine in and that you should become my guests for this evening. We have a great deal to talk over."

"The resolution is carried with acclamation," said Goron. "Monsieur Verneuil must be an unrivalled guide for this part of Paris. I suggest that we place ourselves unreservedly in his hands."

It was not surprising that the conversation at their table should have turned to the subject of drugs. Goron recounted to Verneuil their adventures at St Malo.

"That's the worst of our provincial police system in France," said Verneuil. "The mayor is responsible for the municipal police and if someone buys him over...Then you must remember that these drug traffickers can afford to bribe heavily."

"You must know," said Goron, "that our English friend here is a walking encyclopaedia on the subject. He is the personage who is in charge of the traffic at Scotland Yard and he is sent out to Geneva to represent his country whenever the subject is discussed."

"Indeed! Then perhaps he can solve a good many of our difficulties in Paris."

"I take no credit to myself for knowing something about it, monsieur," said Vincent. "It chanced that the Central Narcotics Intelligence Bureau came across a certain Monsieur Voyatsis and took the liberty of making a search of his baggage. In this certain papers were found which were handed over to me. They included a pocketbook and a code book.

The code book was a compendium of all the persons in China and Japan to whom Voyatsis was in the habit of sending telegrams. On the first page was a list of names of the members of the gang, together with the names of the factories which supplied the poison, for example the Société Industrielle de Chimie Organique and Roessler of Mulhouse."

Verneuil wrinkled up his eyes until they were the merest slits.

"Then it was due to your information that we were able to close those two, which were the most active of our drug manufacturers."

"And what about Hédouin—the name that was in Madame Germaine's book."

"That has been under suspicion for some time, but it is difficult to get direct evidence against the firm. Now, perhaps, we can get a move on."

"Were there no European names?" asked Goron.

"None; probably these were contained in another book which has never come into our hands. In my belief these two Americans about whom we are so much concerned are merely runners—that is they carry the drugs between France and England and France and America."

"And what do you think are the duties of Madame Germaine in the business?"

"She supplies the means of transport. In her case it is hats. Every kind of ingenious device has been pressed into the service. For example, a considerable quantity was concealed in millstones, hollowed out and plastered up so that the stones had to be broken before the drugs could be discovered."

"Now I understand the part played by the wives of the two men: they were employed to buy the hats," said Goron.

"Yes, and I doubt whether their parts were important enough to justify us in following them and searching their rooms. The main thing is that we now have the sources of the supply; what we want to find out is the headquarters of the organization in this country," said Verneuil.

"And I," said Vincent ruefully, "am less concerned with the drug traffic than I am with locating and procuring the arrest of those two men, not on the charge of drug trafficking, but on that of murder." His forehead was wrinkled; he had something on his mind. "Let me be quite frank, Goron. In England, as you know, we cannot arrest people unless we have more than a suspicion that they are concerned in a felony, but in France you are not so strait-laced in your view of these powers. You can arrest on suspicion."

Verneuil's anatomy was disturbed by an eruption of silent laughter. Before Goron could reply he had supplied the answer. "In practice, my friend, and it is only practice that counts, we can arrest anyone. The only risk is that if he's entirely innocent, he may make a fuss, but generally he is so well content to be set at liberty that he says nothing."

A waiter behind Vincent's chair was showing signs of impatience. The other clients had departed a full quarter of an hour earlier. The two French guests took the hint and rose to take their leave.

"*Au revoir* until eight o'clock tomorrow, then," said Verneuil.

Goron and his English colleague met actually on the stairs of the police post at the Grand Palais next morning.

"What a gift is punctuality!" exclaimed Goron, looking at his watch. "We are on the stroke of eight, and here, if I mistake not, comes our colleague Verneuil himself. I recognize his light footfall." It was thus that he described his colleague's heavy tread on the stairs above.

After the usual morning salutations, Vincent enquired how they were to go to the laundry.

"As time presses we will take a taxi," said Verneuil.

"There are not many to be found at this hour, but I have rung up the depot."

He had scarcely finished speaking when a taxi drew up beside them; it had come in response to the telephone message. Verneuil gave the driver the address and they all bundled into it.

By a friendly arrangement with the concierge the three police officers were accorded a position in the courtyard which gave them a view of everyone who passed into the building. A number of women passed in; none was in the least like Madame Germaine. They waited still a few minutes and as there were no new arrivals Verneuil crossed over to a little window at which he had seen all the women record their arrival. The woman behind the glass he recognized as the proprietor's wife. It was no moment for finesse. He asked her bluntly whether all her employees were now in.

"Yes, monsieur," she replied in a sullen tone.

"Then my colleague and I would like to see them at work."

"You will have first to give them time to get into their overalls. Are you looking for anyone in particular?"

"Yes, for the woman who escaped in one of your laundry baskets; you know perfectly well who I mean."

The woman allowed what she hoped to be taken for crass stupidity to pervade her countenance. "I do not know in the least what you mean."

"Well," said Verneuil, "you will know it when we have been through your workers, and if we don't find the woman among them we shall have to search your flat."

"You people seem to do whatever you like," grumbled the woman as she led the way into the sorting room. There, there were only two women, but in the ironing room there were ten. None of these corresponded in the least with the description of Madame Germaine.

Meanwhile Vincent was quietly counting the women in each room. He whispered to Goron at the door of the next room in which nine women were washing: "I counted only twenty women who came in and there are now twenty-one at work."

The women at the washtubs had their hair tucked into mob caps and large coarse aprons enveloped their figures. It would have been an effective disguise for the beautifully groomed milliner of whom they were in search. Vincent was concerned not with their faces or figures, but with their hands. He noticed one whose hands were not wrinkled. He stopped in front of her and made an unobtrusive signal to Goron and Verneuil.

Verneuil addressed the woman: "You must be finding this work hard and distasteful, madame."

The woman behaved as if she had not heard him and went on with her work with redoubled energy.

"You can now drop this disguise, Madame Germaine, and come with me. I am, as you know, an officer from the Prefecture of Police."

She dried her hands on her apron and said with dignity: "I think you will agree, gentlemen, that we cannot discuss things in this room. I suggest that we ask the proprietress to lend us her office for our interview."

She led the way and the three officers followed her. The proprietress was still in the office.

"The curtain has fallen on our farce, *chéri*," said Madame Germaine; "perhaps you will allow these gentlemen to come in and make their explanations."

Once inside the room she removed first the coarse apron and then an overall, revealing a graceful figure in ordinary morning dress. Lastly she removed the mob cap and then all doubts about her identity were removed.

"Are you taking me far?" she asked in polite tones. "Because, if so, I must run upstairs for my hat."

"We'll send for your hat," said Verneuil, bluntly. "You may not want it for some time."

"You mean that I am to be taken to prison?"

"You will be taken to a place where they supply coverings for the head."

She flushed. "This is an outrage. Of what am I accused?"

"I understand that the charge is trafficking in drugs, but all that can be discussed at the place to which you are going."

"You have no right to take me. No doubt you have searched my shop and, naturally, without result. I have never had drugs there."

"May I suggest, madame," said Goron, "that an innocent woman does not escape from her shop in a laundry basket."

"That was a theatrical joke on my part. You were having my shop watched, although you had no grounds for suspicion. I knew you expected a *dénouement* and so I gave you one. Also it gave me an opportunity for showing that your subordinates are not from the top drawer in the matter of intelligence."

"I fear that you will have now to pay for the fun you have had," said Goron. Turning to Verneuil he said: "We will leave you to escort this lady, comrade."

As the two friends left Vincent said: "But you forget that I must get from that woman the addresses of those two men and I must follow them up with all haste and get back to London."

"Have no fear, Vincent. We may safely leave that to Verneuil, who has his own rather rough-and-ready methods of getting the truth out of people, and you might not approve of them. We will call on him later in the day. Meanwhile I am sure that Verneuil will not object to our going round to see whether the postman has dropped any other letter into Madame Germaine's letter box. The man who is keeping observation will be able to tell us."

They walked to the rue Duphot and Goron engaged the watcher in conversation. He said that no one had visited the shop except the little employee who came each morning to see if her employer had returned and couldn't understand her absence.

"I suppose that Verneuil is satisfied that the employee knows nothing," said Vincent.

"Yes, and if Verneuil is satisfied we can take that as proved. It takes much to satisfy Verneuil; he has a distrustful nature."

The man who was keeping observation opened the shop door for them, telling them that the postman had dropped a letter in the box.

The letter bore a London postmark and was addressed to:

Madame Lewis,
> *chez* Madame Germaine, *Modiste*,
>> rue Duphot.

Goron did not scruple to tear the envelope open. The letter was in French, written in an uneducated hand. It ran as follows:

DEAR MADAME,
Please ask your husband to bring a double supply when he comes on August 1st.

Accept, dear madame, the expression of my most devoted sentiments.

ALICE DODDS.

"What address does she give?" asked Vincent eagerly.

"None."

"Then give me the envelope." He examined the postmark, which was not very clear, but he was able to make out W.ll. "I must get back to London at once. August 1st is the day after tomorrow."

"But not without seeing Verneuil?"

"No. I'll make my preparations and be at his office at two o'clock. Will that be convenient to you?"

"Quite. You take the letter. *Au revoir*, at two o'clock."

Chapter Thirteen

WHEN VINCENT ARRIVED at the rendezvous he found Goron waiting at the bottom of the stairs; Verneuil had not yet returned from lunch.

"I should be glad if you'd give me an expert opinion on this letter," said Vincent; "as you see it is written in an illiterate hand, but the composition of the text strikes me as being anything but illiterate, considering that French is a foreign language to the writer."

Goron studied the letter and handed it back. "The handwriting is certainly illiterate, but I judge that the letter has been copied from a text supplied to the writer by a well-educated woman."

"That coincides with my opinion. At any rate I will try to locate Alice Dodds as soon as I get to London and get from her some information about Lewis."

"Alice Dodds may not be easy to find," suggested Goron. "You have only a postmark giving the postal district."

"Quite true, but there is a division of police in each of these postal districts and through them I shall find the woman."

Verneuil entered the lobby at this moment and greeted them in his usual petty officer's manner. They climbed the stairs to his office and when the door was shut Goron enquired without preamble: "Did she talk?"

"Yes, at great length. She gave me information, but I doubt whether any of it was true. According to her version she did nothing in this business but supply hats to the wives of those two men. They were exacting clients—returning over and over again for trifling alterations in the trimmings. When I pointed out that their requirements amounted to converting ribbons, she said that she had nothing to do with the eccentricities of her customers. She admitted having received letters at her shop for them but it was natural for her to oblige customers in this way. Finally, my friends, I decided that if we were to get any further a short sojourn at La Roche would be the only method of persuasion."

"Your method was an inspiration," said Goron, "but we are to lose our British colleague almost immediately."

"Impossible!" said Verneuil. "Just at this moment when our efforts are so soon to be crowned with success. Surely your chiefs can spare you a little longer."

"It is that I have another clue to follow in London. This drug business seems to have wide ramifications, but as you know my main task is to discover the whereabouts of those two Americans. This clue may help." He handed the letter found in Madame Germaine's letter box to the ex-petty officer, who read it with growing excitement.

"A double quantity on the first of August? I suppose that you will take steps on your side of the Channel to intercept this merchandise."

"Indeed we will."

"Of course, we have given orders to all the French ports about these two men, but that is not to say that they won't slip through. Duprez is not the only man who has a fast motorboat."

"I shall arrange for orders to be circulated on our side of the Channel, but, as you say, these motorboats can slip in anywhere."

"Well," said Goron, "your plans are settled and while you're away we shall not be inactive on our side. You remember that the mayor of St Malo told us of a deputy who was protecting these young people, for a consideration that is well understood. We must make it our business to find this gentleman and hear what he has to say on the subject."

"That will be a task for you, my friend," said Verneuil. "Deputies are quite outside my province; they require delicate handling."

"Very well," said Goron; "I will occupy myself with the search for him and also I will send instructions to the Sûreté officer stationed at Cannes to interview those two women and see what he can get out of them."

"If you should come across the tracks of their husbands I hope you will not fail to send me a telegram," said Vincent; "and if I find them I shall, of course, let you know at once."

They parted with mutual expressions of good will. Vincent, who had already booked his passage by air, was in time to catch the afternoon airplane to Croydon. He had telegraphed to Sergeant Walker asking him to meet the plane at Croydon and bring with him the latest reports bearing on the case in which they were interested.

"I have a car here," said the sergeant.

"Very good; then we will talk as we go."

"Well, I haven't been idle while you were away. I have been interviewing the bank officials. Pitt's defalcations amounted to a large sum. The enquiries are not yet complete, but he had certainly made away with a good many thousand pounds. On the other hand, the amount was not large enough to cover the expenses he incurred in his way of living and we've been wondering whether he had not got some other source of supply."

"He had," said Vincent. "I discovered that while I was abroad. He was dealing in drugs."

Sergeant Walker whistled. "That explains a good many things. In following up the tracks of Bernard Pitt, of Hampstead, I found that he had another banking account at the National Insurance Bank, which account he closed on the day before he was murdered. The money was paid to him in Bank of England notes, of which the numbers were known, and one of these notes for ten pounds was brought into a Hammersmith bank and changed for treasury notes. The woman who brought it was made to sign her name on the back—Alice Dodds."

It was now Vincent's turn to whistle. "This is a lucky coincidence. I am hunting that woman at this moment. Have you found her?"

"No, not yet; the information reached me only half an hour ago. Why are you interested in Alice Dodds, Chief Inspector?"

Vincent gave him a brief account of his own doings in Paris. "This woman must be found and made to account for the possession of that note. A C.I.D. officer at Holland Park will do that for us; you see the postal district is W.ll. Will you attend to that part of the enquiry while I am seeing Chief Constable Richardson? You can take this letter."

"I'll drive you straight to the Yard and then go on to Holland Park. You'll be in time to catch the chief constable; he very seldom leaves his table before eight o'clock."

On being admitted to his chief's room, Vincent delivered all the polite messages from France with which he had been charged by Verneuil.

"My friend Verneuil is a rough diamond, but he has a warm heart and an unrivalled knowledge of the French criminal, particularly the Parisian variety. How did he strike you?"

"Well, sir, I can't imagine how he would behave in a drawing room, but he is a good man for a British police officer to know. He can be very useful."

When Richardson had heard his chief inspector's report, he said: "Of course, you did quite right in coming over, but I don't think that those two men that we want will venture to set foot in this country. I agree with you that the woman Dodds must be found; she may prove to be very useful to us. Have you any other plan to work upon now you have come back?"

"Yes, I thought of rounding up the friends of the murdered man—that is, Bernard Pitt, of Hampstead. He must have been supplying some of them with drugs and they might very well give shelter to Blake and Lewis now that the country is getting too hot to hold them."

"You have, of course, warned the port officers?"

"Yes, Sergeant Walker is doing that, but they won't try to come in in the ordinary way; they will come in a motorboat and may land anywhere."

"What about the coast guard?"

"Sergeant Walker is seeing to that also."

"Yes, because it is quite possible that one of the coast guard may spot this motorboat and report the landing of these people. They would, of course, be passed on to the police as having landed illegally, but we ought to be told of it."

"The Newquay police got into touch with their local coast guard about the motorboat that the two men escaped in, but so far no information has come in."

"You have seen Sergeant Walker and he has posted you in the developments on this side of the Channel?"

"Yes sir, he has. My present idea is to get hold of the servants who were at the Hampstead house— the man Anton for choice and the chauffeur."

Richardson consulted the file of papers lying on his table. "This is the file of the Bernard Pitt case and it gives all the information we have. You had better run through it."

"Very good, sir, I will. The dead man's chauffeur is the person most likely to be able to give me the information I want—the names and addresses of Pitt's associates. I did not interview one of his friends at the beginning of the case, but in the light of the drug-traffic information I ought to see others."

"That's the right line of enquiry. See if we have his address in that file; I haven't yet had time to go through it."

Vincent took the file and ran through it with a practised eye. "I see by this that Anton has been allowed to remain in the Hampstead house as a kind of caretaker. I suppose we shall have to pay him something out of 'incidentals.'"

"Yes, he can't live on air."

"I don't see the chauffeur's address in this file, but no doubt Anton will be able to give it to me when I see him. I shall go straight out to Hampstead now."

Vincent did not stop to pick up Sergeant Walker. He took a taxi straight out to the house in Hampstead and rang the bell. Anton, who answered it, was wearing a worried look.

"The telephone has been ringing many times today," he said. "Some ask for Mr Blake and some for Mr Lewis. I tell them they are not here, but oh, sir, it is anxious work for me all alone in this big house. This was not what I came to England for."

"No, but you will have to endure it for a little longer, my friend," said Vincent.

"I ask myself why these people ring up Mr Blake and Mr Lewis when it is known now that my master, their friend, is dead."

"Probably they think that these men, Blake and Lewis, may be hiding in this house now that it is empty. I suppose that none of these people would give their names?"

"No sir, though I always ask them; some of them were ladies."

"You told me the other day that your master never entertained ladies. Are you quite sure of this?"

"Quite sure, sir. If he entertained ladies it must be at some restaurant."

"I suppose the chauffeur will be able to tell me more about these visits to restaurants."

Anton gave a short laugh. "That chauffeur could tell you, sir, but he will not speak. He never speak to anyone and he has no friends. He hated all of us."

"Do you know where he is now?"

"No, he told no one where he was going. All the others, I know where to find them, but not that chauffeur."

"The car is still in the garage?"

"Oh, yes sir; nobody take the car out: the police have the key of the garage."

Just then the telephone bell began to ring persistently. Vincent quickly made up his mind on a course of action.

"Answer the call and if they ask for Mr Blake or Mr Lewis, say that you will call them and come for me."

He listened to the half-conversation.

"I can call Mr Lewis to the telephone, madam, if you hold on." With frantic dumb play Anton signalled to Vincent, who among his other accomplishments could talk American.

He went to the instrument and cried: "Hallo!"

A woman's voice answered: "Is that you?" It was a quavering voice, shaken with emotion of some kind, and without waiting for the answer she went on eagerly: "Have you got it?"

In his best American accent Vincent replied: "I must know who you are."

"Oh, you know, I'm Dodds—Alice Dodds. I want it for myself and her as well. God knows we want it badly enough."

Vincent realized that this woman was in a state in which drug addicts throw caution to the winds. He answered: "Come round to this house right now."

"It'll take me a good part of an hour to make the journey."

"Never mind; I'll wait for you."

He put down the receiver and turned to Anton. "A lady is coming to see me. If the telephone bell rings again do not answer. Let them go on ringing."

"Very good, sir."

"Meanwhile I am going to look over the house again."

Vincent did not expect to make any fresh discovery, but he always found that bodily activity of some kind stimulated thought. These continual telephone messages, what did they mean? Obviously Blake and Lewis must have given the dead man's Hampstead address as a rendezvous and that meant that they intended to use the house, which they supposed would be empty, as a hiding place. If that theory was correct they would first ring up to make sure that the house was empty; that was why he had given Anton the order not to answer the phone. By the letter from Alice Dodds found in Madame Germaine's letter box it was clear that the men were expected on August 1st, and this was July 31st. Almost he began to wish that he had not taken steps to have the men stopped at whatever port they came to, but it was now too late to rescind the order.

Having made a perfunctory second search of the house without result he went down to the ground floor and rang the bell for Anton.

"As I told you, I am expecting a lady. When she comes, go to the door, and if she asks for Mr Lewis show her into the dining room and fetch me. I shall be in that little smoking room opposite."

He had not long to wait. His visitor had been better than her word. When the bell rang Anton followed his instructions, showed the visitor into the dining room and fetched Vincent.

She was a walking example of what addiction to heroin will reduce a self-respecting woman to. It was obvious from her speech that she belonged to the upper servant class, but she was ill dressed and untidy in her person and there was an air of entire indifference to her appearance. She did not rise when he entered the room, but looked at him with lacklustre eyes.

"Where's Mr Lewis and who are you?"

"I'm here to see you instead of Mr Lewis."

A dark cloud of distrust and suspicion was evident in her expression. "Has he let me down?"

"You mean, has he failed to bring what you expected?"

"He's got it all right, but he wants to frighten me into paying more than the regular rate. He thinks that she will always pay anything he chooses to ask."

Vincent realized that this lack of caution was characteristic of the addict in the later stages. She had taken it for granted that he was one of Lewis's associates. He decided to drop all play-acting, together with his assumed American accent.

"Mr Lewis is not here, madam, but now that you have come I have some questions to ask you."

Her attitude changed: she shook with fear, not the fear of being questioned, but the fear that she was not going to receive what she had come for.

"When do you expect him here?" she said with a kind of wail in her tone.

"We'll talk about Mr Lewis later on. First I want you to answer my questions. Why did you expect Mr Lewis to be here?"

"Because he answered the telephone."

"Why did you telephone to him here?"

"Because his letter said this house on August 1st and to-morrow is the first. She said he might arrive earlier."

"Who is she?"

"I'm not going to answer your questions," she said rudely.

"Very well, just as you like, only unless you do you'll have to come with me to the police station."

"No, don't take me there," she said, cringing with alarm. "They took *her* there once when she was put on probation and she's never forgotten it. She went through hell."

"Is she your mistress?"

"She was once, but I'm not in service now." She assumed a boastful air. "I'm a lady living on my own now."

Vincent decided to adopt another method of attack. "Who gave you that ten-pound note which you changed for treasury notes at the bank in Holland Park?"

"Oh, I picked it up in the street, and finding's keeping, you know."

"When you pick up valuable property in the street you should take it to the nearest police station."

"Oh, I can't be bothered with all these silly rules. I often pick up money in the streets." She went on to recount wild stories of wealth she had picked up in the gutter; of jewels worth a fortune dropped by ladies getting out of taxis. Vincent gave her five minutes with her imagination and then began to question her again. For another five minutes he plied her patiently, but with no good result. Sometimes she behaved as if she hadn't heard him.

"Did you hear what I said?" he asked.

"Yes, but I can't be bothered answering questions."

Vincent decided that the proper course was to take her to the police station and let the police surgeon deal with her. He went to the door and signalled to Anton.

"Ring up a taxi," he whispered, "and when it arrives, come in and announce it. I shall take this lady away, but I shall come back because I intend to spend the night here."

To Vincent's great relief the woman followed him to the taxi without demur. He gave the address of the nearest police station and they drove off together.

Chapter Fourteen

THE POLICE SURGEON was sent for and while the woman was in charge of the matron Vincent explained the situation to the doctor.

"Of course, you know all about the symptoms of drug addicts when they have been deprived of their favourite poison."

"I ought to; if I don't it is not from lack of practice."

"Well, I have questions to put to this woman and I can get nothing out of her in her present state. She can be held for the present on another charge: she was in possession of a stolen ten-pound note."

"Very good. I'll see to her and I'll ring you up as soon as she is in a state where she can usefully be questioned. I suppose if I ring up the Yard you will get the message?"

"Yes," said Vincent. "I'm going back there immediately, but I may not be able to stop there long."

"Oh, that's all right. The woman will sleep here tonight and I shan't want you until the morning."

Vincent found Walker in the sergeants' room at the Yard and called him into the chief inspectors' room.

"You and I have got a busy night before us. We'll have to take it in turns to keep watch in that house at Hampstead, because it is quite possible that our American friends, thinking the house empty, will take the liberty of breaking in: it will save a deal of trouble if they do. Anton tells me that the telephone bell has been busy and I think that the clients are expecting those two, and that they have been given that address."

"Unless they've already landed, I think they'll have difficulty in getting through. I have warned the coast guard people as well as the port officers and there 'll be a sharp lookout everywhere."

"Then we'll be off and trust to Anton to provide us with some kind of meal."

Anton proved himself to be a skilled chef. He provided them with a meal worthy of a first-class restaurant. The two officers kept alternate watch during the night, but it passed off uneventfully. Police officers are accustomed to disappointments of this kind; neither was depressed by the failure of their hopes. Anton provided them with hot baths and breakfast before they made for the Yard.

On Vincent's table lay two telegrams, one from Goron to say that the two women had left Cannes and, not improbably, would attempt to enter England; the other from the coast guard at Newquay saying that a motorboat had landed two men and two women in Pulsey Cove in the early hours of the morning and they were being detained by the Newquay police on the charge of landing illegally.

Vincent leapt from his chair and made a dash for the door of the sergeants' room to find Walker. The sergeants, engaged in writing up their reports, were accustomed to these sudden irruptions: Vincent had a reputation throughout the service of being a man who could not take life easily.

"I want you, Walker. Come along to my room."

They were alone in the chief inspectors' room and Vincent was free to indulge his instinct for quick movement. He paced up and down.

"Here, Walker, read these." He handed him the telegrams. "There'll be no mayor to connive at their escape on this side of the Channel, thank the Lord. But you and I will have to go down to Newquay immediately; otherwise the local beaks may dismiss them with a caution."

"Won't the Aliens' Department at the Home Office have something to say?"

"They may, but they're funny people at the Home Office. It depends upon whose hand the papers fall into. While you are getting the car round and filling her up I'll telephone to the doctor at Hampstead about that woman, Alice Dodds."

The police surgeon at Hampstead had a callous manner of dealing with such cases.

"We've got the woman in cold storage, but you know what it is with addicts when the supply is suddenly cut off. She has all the symptoms of reaction, vomiting, sneezing, sweating and palpitation of the heart. It will be some days before she will be fit to be questioned."

"Were any papers found in her handbag, or concealed about her person, because I've reason to believe she has been acting for a person in a much higher social position."

"Nothing was found on her, except her name and address and a sum of eighty pounds in treasury notes."

"Will you give me her address and I'll have inquiries made about her in the division."

He made a note of the address and before Sergeant Walker returned he had time to send a note to the division requesting that a report should be made to him on the woman's mode of life. By that time the car was waiting for him. Vincent took the wheel himself; it was to be a long run and a fast one.

At Newquay police station they saw Inspector Harrowby, the officer who was in charge of the car in which Bernard Pitt had apparently been murdered.

"You are holding four people on a charge of landing illegally," said Vincent.

"We are—two men and two women. They have told us the usual kind of fairy tale, that the captain was a personal friend and that it seemed to be the cheapest way of coming. We've submitted the case to the Aliens' Department at the Home Office and are awaiting instructions. If it is decided not to prosecute, they will be taken in custody to the nearest port and pushed out."

"I want them for something else. It may interest you to know that they were the men who left that motorcar behind when they left Newquay a few days ago."

"Do you think they were coming back for the car?"

"No. I think their plan was to make for the nearest railway station and take the train to London. Have they been searched?"

"They have. They were carrying personal luggage but nothing contraband."

"An excessive amount of luggage?"

"Nothing out of the way. Would you like to see them?"

"Yes, I should—one at a time and the women first. Let each one bring her luggage in with her."

Mrs Blake was the first to come in carrying a suitcase of moderate size. She was tall and rather handsome. Vincent judged her to be a little on the wrong side of thirty. She spoke English with a very slight foreign accent.

"You are the customs officer, no doubt," she said, with a charming smile. "We did not know that we were committing a grave crime in landing as we did. We happened to know the captain of the motorboat and begged him to give us a passage, but you can examine everything we brought with us, just as if we had landed at Dover or Folkestone."

She opened her suitcase with alacrity. "You see there is nothing here, but one change of clothes, which any woman would need."

"I see," said Vincent, dryly; "and of course a second hat."

"Of course," she agreed.

"I am particularly interested in the hat, also in the one you have on your head. May I ask you to remove it and let me look at it."

She looked a little disconcerted, but she did as he asked with the best grace she could muster.

"You see," he explained with a smile, "I happen to know your milliner in Paris. Madame Germaine."

"Ah! Madame Germaine is a *modiste* of talent."

"I must ask you to step into this room," he said, politely opening the door for her, "while I see your friend. Your hats will be safe in my keeping."

He closed the door behind her and put her hats in a cupboard before sending for Mrs Lewis.

Mrs Lewis was a contrast to her friend. She was small and slight and her foreign accent was more pronounced. She said that she had been born in Austria and began a voluble explanation of her reasons for coming into England in a motorboat.

Vincent stemmed the flood by putting up his hand firmly. She seemed to think that he was going to stop her mouth with a large hand and she subsided into a few broken sentences.

"I know exactly what you were going to tell me," he said. "Your friend has already given the explanation which you made up between you. It is your luggage that interests me. Kindly put it down and remove your hat. Thank you."

Vincent's rough-and-ready way of dealing with her dried up the springs of eloquence. Tears came into her eyes and here again Vincent opposed the cold douche of brutality which he had assumed.

"If you wish to cry, madam, I would ask you not to do it in this room. You can cry on your friend's shoulder." He threw open the door and motioned her into the next room. It was as if he had swept her out with a broom.

He opened the door into the passage and called in the inspector. "I have a job here which only a woman can do," he said. "You see these hats—four of them. I've reason to believe that the trimmings are tubular and contain drugs. Have you anyone who can unpick them carefully and put the contents of each trimming into a separate envelope for analysis?"

The inspector wrinkled his brow. "I doubt whether the police matron would be up to a job like this; she has a fist like a prize fighter, but we'll try her, if you like."

But when the matron was called she tossed her head at the idea that there had been any doubt about her competence. Any woman, it appeared, could do what was wanted, and she took from her bag the scissors and other tools necessary and then and there began to dissect a hat.

"I'm sure the inspector will provide you with some stout envelopes for the job, if you will take the hats downstairs with you."

The next task was to interview the two men separately. Blake was called first. He was a stout, thick-set man with a protruding under jaw. His manner proclaimed the fact that he was an American who feared neither man nor devil and who had a contempt for the legal machinery of a foreign country. Vincent knew the type.

"I suppose you haven't come back for your car?" he said.

"What's that?"

Vincent repeated his question, which appeared little to the man's taste.

"Why..."

"You needn't trouble to think out a reply. It would tire your brain to make up a plausible story, but I can save you the trouble. We know what has brought you here; you were bringing merchandise for people in London which would not have passed the customs. Unfortunately for you in landing it like this you have broken the law doubly, but I have a few questions to ask you about the car you left behind on your last visit."

"You've got the wrong man, mister. I know nothing about a car and I defy you to find anything in my baggage that you can hold me on."

"No, the contraband was carried by the ladies in their hats, but I must warn you that you may have a more serious charge to answer—a charge of wilful murder. I must caution you that anything you say will be taken down and may be used in subsequent proceedings."

"See here, boss, you're barking up the wrong tree. I want to save you trouble hereafter. What the women were carrying was no concern of mine. They happen to know the captain of that boat and he offered to run us all over and land us. As to a motorcar and wilful murder, you're talking through your hat."

"The garagist here in Newquay with whom you left the car and the owner who hired it to you and your friend, Mr Bernard Pitt, will be able to identify you."

The man proceeded to make the American eagle scream. Vincent cut him short by rising and opening the door. "You can finish the rest of your harangue downstairs. I have no time to listen to it. Inspector," he called, "take this man downstairs and send up the other."

The second man, Lewis, was of a different type. He was older and less blatant. Moreover, he had a story to tell at the end of the first five minutes. He did not deny having left the car.

"See here," he said quietly, "we didn't come back for that car and you know why. There had been murder done in it."

"I'd better warn you that you are suspected of murder and that anything you say will be taken down and may be used hereafter."

"Oh, I know all about that. You needn't worry yourself. We didn't commit that murder, but I know we shall have a job in getting you guys to believe it."

"If you would like to make a statement, I'll call my sergeant and get him to take it down in writing and then you can sign it."

"O.K. Call him in."

As soon as Walker was in his place with his note-book and pencil, the man began. As he listened to the story Vincent reflected that it was the most incredible story that he had ever listened to and that it did credit to the imagination of the man who told it.

"I guess that you know a good deal of what I'm going to tell you, but there it is. I'll tell you the truth and you can make what you like of it. It was a week ago last Saturday when my friend Blake and I started off with Bernard Pitt for Newquay in a car that he'd hired for the journey; we were to meet a motorboat belonging to a friend of ours which was to take us over to France. We hadn't gone far out of town when a man jumped out of a car ahead and stuck out his arms to stop us. He was got up to look like a regular bandit as you see in the flicks. Pitt was sitting at the back alone; the bandit got in beside him, fired and jumped out again. It was all so sudden, that we hadn't time to do anything. We didn't realize at first that Pitt had been killed. At that moment a terrific thunderstorm started. It got so bad that we couldn't go on. We saw a barn a little way off the main road and made up our minds to shelter in it, but the car was too big to get in. It was then we discovered that Pitt was dead, and Blake said: 'It won't do for us to be found with a dead man in the car; we'd better take him out and dump him; nobody will see us in a storm like this.' Then we went on to Newquay."

"But you stopped on the way to get the broken window taken out."

"Yes, that was Blake's idea. He's always getting brain waves like that. He nearly lost us the boat through that one."

"Why didn't you give information to the police at the time? Your story was more likely to be believed then than it is now."

"I know it, but you see in my country the cops are out to make a bit on every deal and a quick getaway is the safest."

"Bernard Pitt was escaping from the country with a large sum of stolen money on him. What became of that?"

"It was taken by the bandit I told you of."

"You said that he was in a car. What sort of car was it?"

"Sure I can't tell you that. I've told you that it all happened so quickly that it took our wits away. I could swear it was a dark colour and that's all."

"What happened to the bandit?"

"He jumped back into his car and got away. He drove like hell."

"Well, you are now under arrest for importing narcotics into this country."

"We were fools to come back here; we were safer in France."

"In France you had powerful protection."

"Why, certainly, but the protection was paid for."

"It was no less a person than a deputy?"

"You mean Monsieur Laurillard? Why yes, but I guess he can do nothing for us in this darned country."

"Surely you've squared someone over here?"

"We thought we had squared the Newquay coast guard, but they were pulling our legs."

"Thank you. That's all I have to ask you for the moment. You must consider yourself under arrest. Now, Walker," he said, as soon as the door was closed, "get this wire sent off to Goron, Ministry of the Interior, Paris. Name of the deputy is Laurillard, and sign it Vincent."

Chapter Fifteen

ON RECEIVING Vincent's telegram, Goron looked up the private address of M. Laurillard and decided that seven o'clock at night was an inauspicious hour for a momentous interview with a deputy. It was the dinner hour and a gentleman of that standing would not be found in the bosom of his family at home. Most probably he was dining with his friends either at the Chamber itself or in a restaurant nigh at hand. It would be better to defer the interview until the morning, when he would have the whole day before him for anything that might happen.

It was ten o'clock the following morning when he rang the bell at the Laurillard flat and handed his card to the manservant. He had time to observe that the flat was expensively furnished in the modern style.

He had not long to wait, probably no longer than sufficed for the gentleman to decide upon the replies he was to make if he was questioned about his connection with the drug traffic, because a man who was engaged in risky transactions such as his must always feel that the axe was hanging over his head.

"I have called to give you a hint, monsieur; some friends of yours in this country and in England are in danger and may require you to use all the influence you possess on their behalf."

The flabby complexion of the deputy took on a sicklier shade. "I do not understand to whom you are referring," he stammered.

"No? Then let me make things plainer. Persons concerned in illegally introducing narcotics into England and this country have been arrested and they are counting upon you to restore them to liberty."

"You speak as if I was a Court of Appeal. I have no power to have them released." He drew himself up with dignity and continued: "Really, this is an outrage. I must bring it to the notice of my friend, the minister. How dare you suggest that I, a deputy in the Chamber, am linked with scoundrelly traffickers in drugs."

"I fear that you must blame your friends rather than me, and if I may be permitted to give you a word of advice, I suggest that you would be making a mistake in appealing for protection to the minister. I am merely carrying out my duty in calling upon you."

Laurillard had been doing some rapid thinking; his manner changed. "It is not worth troubling the minister with so trumpery a charge. I will interview these people who dare to abuse my name."

"Unfortunately two of them named Blake and Lewis have been detained in England by the British authorities."

"The mistakes made by the British police have nothing to do with me. Who is there in France that I can deal with?"

Goron decided that for the time at least it would be prudent to withhold the name of the mayor of St Malo. "There is a milliner in the rue Duphot named Madame Germaine..."

"A woman? Send her to me and let me deal with her."

"If you will come with me to the police station at the Grand Palais, I will have her brought to you."

"I cannot come at once. I have to be at the Chamber."

"We will make any time you choose convenient. Shall we say this evening at half-past five?"

"Very good; that time will do. I will come to the Grand Palais."

Goron's next objective was the office of his friend Verneuil. To him he narrated his receipt of the telegram and his interview with Laurillard.

"Ah! So M. Laurillard was the protector and friend of this little gang." He began to chuckle. The tremor began low down in his anatomy and worked its way upwards until it culminated in laughter. "One finds them everywhere, these eager gentlemen who snatch at illicit profits, but most of all among the politicians, for their harvest may be a short one and they make their hay only when the sun is shining.

"Have you loosened the tongue of that woman Germaine?"

Verneuil screwed up his eyes. "Not yet, but I think that an interview between M. Laurillard and her may produce something."

"Then we must contain our curiosity until half past five, when this intriguing interview is to take place."

Goron spent the next few hours in making confidential enquiries about M. Laurillard and his friends and relations. As it proved, his time was not ill spent; he had gleaned some facts that were likely to be useful when the interview took place.

He arrived at the Grand Palais a few minutes before the appointed hour and climbed the stairs to Verneuil's room. There he found Madame Germaine in her full panoply of make-up, beautifully dressed and groomed and bristling with the self-confidence that women enjoy when they feel themselves to be well turned out. She was feeling, like so many of her sex, that men were soft clay in the hands of the potter.

Verneuil, whose whimsical expression Goron knew so well, observed: "Madame Germaine is looking forward to her interview with her old friend, Monsieur Laurillard."

"Yes, indeed," burst out the woman; "now I shall see justice done."

Verneuil bowed obsequiously. "And we shall make our humble apologies for any inconvenience that Madame has suffered."

It was at this moment that M. Laurillard was announced. Madame Germaine rose from her chair and approached him with outstretched hand. He drew back.

"I have not the honour of Madame's acquaintance," he said.

"Oh," said the lady; "so that is to be the line, is it? It is well to know how we stand. I will give you one chance, monsieur, before laying all my cards on the table before these gentlemen. Is this the first time that we have met?"

There was a cold light in her eye which Laurillard could not fail to see. His instinct was to compromise. He turned to the others, saying: "Can I see this lady alone?"

Goron replied: "I cannot see why a private interview should be necessary on the mere question whether you and this lady are acquainted."

"It is possible that this is not the first time that I have met this lady. She might recall the incident to my memory if we could talk *tête-à-tête.*"

Before either of the men had time to reply, Madame Germaine burst forth with blazing eyes: "So you would cast a slur on my character; you would pretend that if we met it was merely a passing love affair. Very well, then. I have borne much and I can bear no more. I am free to tell these gentlemen all that they are anxious to know."

Laurillard made a last attempt to save his face. "Of course you two gentlemen are free to take down any cock-and-bull story that a detractor chooses to make. When the time comes I shall defend my honour. At the moment I have important business to discharge in another part of Paris and I cannot stop to hear her."

Goron placed his back against the door. "You will pardon me, monsieur; I, too, have questions to put to you before you go."

"By what right? I am a deputy. I have my parliamentary duties to attend to..."

"Quite right, monsieur, but my questions will have nothing to do with your parliamentary duties."

"I shall have to make a complaint to my friend, the Minister of the Interior, about this insult on the part of one of his functionaries. You know that as a deputy I am immune from this form of petty persecution."

"I merely wanted to ask you whether M. Charles Laurillard, one of the directors of the Hédouin chemical laboratory in Belfort, is your son."

"He is," burst out Madame Germaine, unable any longer to contain herself. "And this factory turns out the stuff which the Blake and Lewis women have been dealing in."

Laurillard drew himself up. "My son's factory is engaged in important government work."

"Yes, and what about the secret room behind two steel doors? What goes on there?" said Madame Germaine vindictively.

"That," said Laurillard, sinking his voice almost to a whisper, "is the room in which the famous anti-gas product is being made for the masks. She has no right to know about it."

Goron now played his trump card. "Whatever goes on in that secret room is already known to the Sûreté Nationale, who were to pay a visit to it this afternoon."

Laurillard made a final attempt to retreat with dignity. "If it is proved," he said, with lips so dry that they scarcely enunciated the words, "if my son is proved to have done anything contrary to the interests of his country, I shall be among the first to vote for his punishment."

Neither Goron nor Verneuil did more than bow him out. When the door was shut behind him, Verneuil's attitude was trying to Goron's gravity, for half unconsciously he was mimicking the dignified carriage of their late visitor. In fact, thought Goron, my friend Verneuil is a positive loss to the French stage.

"Well now," said Madame Germaine; "you have begun to realize some of the truth, namely that I am guiltless and that the real malefactors are that gentleman and his son Charles."

Goron left Verneuil to answer. "I fear, madame, that the hospitality that I provided for you at La Roche has not been entirely to your liking; you would prefer the comforts of your own home, and if I felt sure that you would stay there without having recourse to a laundry basket, we might come to terms."

"You are going the best way to ruin me, gentlemen. My shop has been closed for days and all my customers will desert me for rival establishments. Surely you've done enough."

"We shall have done enough as soon as you have done something on your side by making a clean breast of your connection with this affair of drug smuggling."

"Very well; I'll tell you. My connection with the affair began when those two ladies came to me to buy hats and insisted that the trimmings should be made tubular. They explained laughingly that they wished to smuggle perfume into England. Later they brought to me some coarse white powder which I was to introduce into trimmings in such a way that it couldn't leak out. I guessed that something was wrong and demurred. After some discussion..."

"And something passing from hand to hand," murmured Verneuil. "After some discussion you consented?"

"Yes, to oblige the ladies."

The ex-petty officer's eyes narrowed to a slit. "It is always worth while to oblige customers, isn't it?"

"Well, of course, that's how commerce goes forward."

"In what other way did you oblige your customers?" asked Goron.

"I did receive letters at my shop for them."

"What did you do with the letters?"

"I had instructions sometimes to forward them, sometimes to hold them till they called."

"But you warned these people when we first made enquiries at your shop. Under whose instructions did you do that?"

"The instructions of M. Laurillard." She brought out the name almost triumphantly.

"When did you first meet this distinguished deputy?"

"Some months ago. I was introduced to him by Madame Lewis. He assured me that I should be safe from molestation by people like you if I consented to act as their post office."

"You knew that they were trafficking in drugs," said Goron.

"To be frank, I guessed it."

"And your friends at the laundry. How came they to be mixed up in this business?"

"Oh, they had no part in this at all. They helped me to escape for old friendship's sake. I had been able to help them in building up their business."

"You were not a very good guardian of correspondence. You took alarm as soon as you saw that your shop was being watched and you left your letter box in the hands of the police."

"Sir, you had me in your power. I was a foreigner and I knew that with a snap of the fingers you could have had me expelled from France and deprived of my livelihood. I had to look after my own skin. As you have learned from your interview with M. Laurillard, he would not have moved a finger to save me."

"Well, madame," said Verneuil, "for the time being you shall be set at liberty, but it is right to warn you that your correspondence will be supervised."

She shrugged her shoulders. "You may not believe me, gentlemen, but my profession is more to me than this wretched business into which I was dragged. If people write foolish letters to me and you intercept them, it will concern them, not me. I shall do nothing but read the letters which you allow the postman to bring to me. All I ask is that you do not expel me from France, the country that I love."

They allowed her to go and Verneuil seized the opportunity for asking how Goron had discovered the identity of Laurillard's son.

"That was simpler than you think. 'Laurillard' is not a very common name. As you know since this affair started, my department has been getting together all possible information about chemical factories in France. I searched through the lists of directors and in one of them I found the name of Laurillard, a director of the Hédouin chemical laboratory in Belfort. As you know, that address was in Germaine's notebook. I made further enquiries and found, as I expected, that this Charles Laurillard was the son of a distinguished deputy. You can put two and two together. I got a move on and arranged for an inspection of this factory and its accounts. That took place this afternoon. You see the connection. The factory turns out narcotics under the pretence that it is making anti-gas chemicals for the government. The son Charles sells the narcotics through a small gang, and M. Laurillard, the distinguished deputy, sits up aloft as their loving friend and protector."

"And," said Verneuil, "pockets a good share of the profits."

"Exactly. Now I think that we know the whole story."

"I gather from the telegram sent by our English friend that he has captured his two murderers. We owe him gratitude for having sent us Laurillard's name."

"During my investigation of the Laurillard family I have today learned something that may interest him. The daughter of the deputy married an Englishman named Pearson and is now living in England. The last letter found in the box of Madame Germaine had a London postmark. It intrigued our English colleague because the writing was illiterate, but the text, which was in French, and the spelling were impeccable. This marriage I speak of may be the explanation. At any rate I shall send him this information and he may hunt up Madame Pearson. I leave you now, my friend, in order to write this letter."

Chapter Sixteen

CHIEF CONSTABLE RICHARDSON had been listening to Vincent's report.

"Where are these two men now?" he asked.

"I presume that they are in prison. They were brought up before the Newquay magistrates who, when they heard how the men had landed and that drugs had been found on the two women, remanded them and refused bail."

"You have not yet charged them with murder?"

"No sir, it is about that that I have come to take your instructions. Their story is fantastic."

"During a long career, Mr Vincent, I have found that even fantastic stories cannot be dismissed with a shrug of the shoulders."

"Circumstantial evidence is all against them. The window of the car was shattered by a bullet; they stopped to have the window replaced, which would have been the instinct of guilty people."

"We must not forget that the first instinct of these drug traffickers is to avoid any contact with the police. Have you any further evidence?"

"Yes sir, I have. A note stolen from the murdered man was changed by a woman named Alice Dodds. This woman is a drug addict and we have a letter signed by her proving that she was in contact with these people."

"Then she is an important witness. Have you found her?"

"Yes." He explained his meeting with the woman in the Hampstead house. "But she is not in a physical condition to be charged or questioned. She has been taken to a cottage hospital, where the matron and the medical superintendent have agreed to notify us as soon as she is fit to be discharged."

"But you have made enquiries about her?"

"I have, sir. She lives in a comfortable little flat in Holland Park and apparently has private means. The housekeeper of the flats could say nothing about her except that she was very delicate and often prostrated by illness. I have told you about the mysterious 'she' whom she frequently mentioned. The housekeeper said that a lady often came in a big car driven by a chauffeur to see Alice Dodds, but she did not know her name. From information I have just received from the Paris police I am inclined to think that the mysterious lady may be a Mrs Pearson—a Frenchwoman married to an Englishman, the daughter of the Paris deputy, M. Laurillard."

"The man mixed up with the drug-trafficking gang. You have not yet located her, I suppose?"

"No sir, but we have the name and we know that she has a Lanchester car. We are making enquiries at the London County Council office for licensing cars. I hope to have her address this afternoon."

"Very good, but in view of the story told by Lewis and Blake, you ought to find out whether the murdered man had ever been threatened. Have you questioned the servants again?"

"I am anxious to find the chauffeur, who would know most about the people visited by his master, but at present no one knows his address."

"Well, hunt him up."

"I have a theory of my own. The dead man frequented card parties, where they played for high stakes. In a second interview I had with Blake he suggested that Pitt was murdered by a man who had lost large sums of money to him and was unable to repay them. As you know, sir, thousands change hands in a single night at these parties."

"That theory sounds good. I see why you want to find the chauffeur."

"There is someone else who might help me—a Mr Brooklyn—in Jermyn Street. I've seen him once and he seemed quite ready to help us if he could. He may be able to furnish the names of people who used to play at these parties."

"Then you had better see him again."

"Very good, sir. I should probably find him at home now."

On leaving his chief's room, Vincent made straight for Jermyn Street. He found Mr Brooklyn home, but their conversation led to nothing useful.

"None of the people that I met at those card parties would have been at all likely to resort to murder to get rid of a gambling debt, except, perhaps, those two Americans, but they did not lose; they won."

"I may tell you that we suspected those Americans and I have questioned them. They told me a fantastic story of having been held up near Oldbury by a masked bandit."

Brooklyn burst out laughing. "You don't mean to say that you, a hard-boiled officer from Scotland Yard, believed a cock-and-bull story like that. Why, man, it was hatched at Hollywood."

"However improbable a story sounds we are trained to investigate it. Only in that way can we arrive at the truth."

"Well, Inspector, that further clears all the people I ever played cards with. Mine were well on the wrong side of middle age and the idea of a masked bandit occurs only to the youth between twenty and thirty." He added with a grin: "I myself plead guilty to being on the wrong side of forty-five."

Vincent joined in his laughter and took his leave, reflecting as he went down the stairs that the theory that the murderer was a young man was the more likely—always providing that there was any truth in the story. His next visit was to Hampstead to see what news Anton could give him. The news was important. The chauffeur had called to know whether the car had been disposed of and Anton had got his address from him.

"Has he another job?" asked Vincent.

"Not yet, he said. He asked me if any ladies had telephoned. I said: 'Why do you think ladies should telephone,' and he said: 'To take up his reference when he applied for a new job.'"

"Did you tell him about the woman who came here?"

"No sir. I think you would wish no one to be told about that."

"Quite right, Anton. No one else has telephoned, I suppose?"

"No, monsieur."

"Well, give me the chauffeur's address and I'll go and see him."

Anton scurried off into the back regions and returned with a slip of paper torn off the margin of a newspaper. Vincent copied the address into his note-book. It was in the neighbourhood of Palmer's Green. As Vincent had the car he drove out there.

It was a small house with a tiny garden in front. A middle-aged woman opened the door.

"Does Mr Arthur Green live here?"

"Yes sir, he is my son. Do you want to see him?"

"Yes, I won't keep him long."

"Come in and I'll call him." She went to the bottom of the stairs and called: "Arthur, you're wanted," and Vincent heard the clatter of boots on the stairs. "It's a gent in the dining room," explained his mother.

The chauffeur looked worse for wear since Vincent had seen him last. He apologized for a three days' growth of beard by saying: "One gets mouldy out of a job. There's nothing to shave for if you understand what I mean."

"Surely you won't be long out of a job."

"In these days there are too many owner-drivers about," replied the man gloomily. "That's why there are so many accidents every week; half of them are unfit to be on the road."

"Some of the accidents are caused by people driving under the influence of drink," said Vincent, looking straight at him. "It's a dangerous thing for a chauffeur to take to."

The man flushed. "I never drink when I'm in regular work, but naturally when one's out of a job with nothing to do..."

"I understand. First one pal and then another asks you in, but take my advice and keep a hold on yourself."

"That's right; I'm going to."

"You used to drive your late master out in the evenings. I want you to give me the names and addresses of people he went to see—to spend the evening with."

"I gave you one—Mr Brooklyn of Jermyn Street."

"Yes, but only one. I want you to give me others. Did you know any of these friends by sight?"

"Yes, some of them."

"Were any of them youngish men?"

"Yes, some of them—Mr Brooklyn, for instance."

"Can you think of anyone else?"

"Mr Thelusson in Arkley Street—number 41."

Vincent jotted it down in his notebook. "Anyone else?"

The chauffeur gave quite a string of names and Vincent noted them all.

"When you were with Mr Pitt did you live in the house?"

"No, I couldn't stick the servants, so Mr Pitt let me have my own rooms over the garage."

"Why didn't you like the servants?"

"Well, they were all blooming foreigners, and I don't trust foreigners."

"Were the keys of your quarters over the garage handed over to the police with the keys of the house?"

"Yes, your sergeant took them when he took all the other keys."

"You have seen a lady recently about a new job?"

"No, I haven't."

"Think again."

The man looked a little uneasy. "Well, I've seen quite a lot of people, but nothing's come of it."

"What made you give the address of your late master as a reference when you knew he was dead?"

"Well, I had to give some address."

"But you knew a dead man couldn't give a reference."

"I said that I'd worked at that address when Mr Pitt was alive."

"I see. Well, if you do get a job you can give me as a reference."

"Thank you, I will."

"Well, thank you for this list of names. I must get on and see the people."

"Have you found the murderer of Mr Pitt yet?"

"Not yet. When we do you'll see it in the papers." Vincent was studying the list of names as he left the house, but he did not visit any of them; he drove back to the Yard to find Sergeant Walker and get from him the key of the garage and the chauffeur's quarters over it.

"You'd better jump up and come with me, Walker, bringing the keys with you. I have a feeling that that chauffeur knows more than he's told us. I didn't take to the man at all."

They drove straight to Hampstead and without communicating with Anton they stopped the car and walked to the garage, which stood out of sight of the house. The car was still there. They made a methodical search of all the pockets but found only an expired insurance policy and a road map. Upstairs the rooms were neat and fairly clean. There was a little stale food in the kitchen cupboard and in the table drawer there were a few papers relating to motorcars and accessories.

"Nothing much here," began Vincent, and then he stopped with a sharp exclamation. "This is interesting! A car licence for a Lanchester car owned by Mrs Pearson."

"It's a common name," observed Walker.

"It is; it would be strange if it turned out to be the Mrs Pearson we are looking for, and, by Jove! It has the lady's address. We may as well call on her at once. This is one of those expensive flats in Piccadilly. I know them. We'll park the car in Berkeley Square and walk."

It was a service flat. The uniformed porter directed them to the third floor and they were admitted to Mrs Pearson's flat. She proved to be a woman in the thirties, and Vincent judged from her surroundings that she had ample means. Although plain in feature, she had a fair share of the chic of her countrywomen and bore no outward signs of being a drug addict.

"I am sorry to trouble you," he said, "but I have to get some information about a chauffeur who was formerly in your employment, named Arthur Green."

"Arthur Green? Yes, he was a good driver and he knew the West End of London fairly well."

"Why did you part with him?"

"He left me of his own accord, saying that as I had told him that I might want him to drive me in France, he would prefer to leave."

"Of course, Madame being French would naturally wish to visit her own country."

"I am English by marriage."

"But M. Laurillard, your father, is French."

"The service to which you belong seems to be loaded with unimportant details. My parentage has nothing to do with my former chauffeur, about whom you have come to enquire."

Vincent smiled enigmatically. "How long ago did he leave you?" he enquired.

"About a year as far as I can remember."

"When he left you I understand that he went to a Mr Bernard Pitt. Did you know Mr Pitt?"

She hesitated for a moment; her hesitation was not lost upon Vincent. "Pitt is not an uncommon name in England."

"I mean Mr Bernard Pitt."

"I knew a Mr Pitt who was cashier at my bank, but not socially."

"Mr Pitt had a large circle of friends who did not know that he was employed in a bank, but you knew him only as a bank cashier?"

"That's all." Behind her apparent indifference Vincent marked an undertone of anxiety.

"I think you know a woman named Alice Dodds."

The lady appeared to search her memory. "Alice Dodds? No. I don't think I've ever heard that name before."

"Was she never employed by you?"

"No, because in that case I should remember her name."

"But your Lanchester car is seen not infrequently at the door of her lodgings."

"Oh, then all I can think of is that my chauffeur drives there occasionally without my permission."

"You would have no objection, I'm sure, to my interviewing your chauffeur."

"Not at all, but it will take some minutes. I have always to call him by telephone when I want him."

"Never mind. I will wait."

"Very well, then I will telephone to him. I will leave the door open; you will like to listen," she added with an arch smile.

She spoke in French very rapidly and Vincent failed to catch anything that might have been construed as a warning. She returned to the room.

"You will like to assure yourself that I have no communication with him before you see him."

She handed him an illustrated magazine and picked up some unfinished embroidery. Ten minutes passed before the chauffeur made his appearance. He was a Frenchman and their conversation was conducted in French. Pressed by Vincent, he made a shame-faced acknowledgment that he had occasionally used his mistress' car without her permission to visit Alice Dodds, whom he had met casually in a little restaurant. He apologized for this breach of decorum to his mistress, who with dignity replied that she would discuss the matter with him at some future time.

Turning to Vincent, she said: "Do you wish to question him any further?"

Vincent shook his head; he had decided not to press either of them any further at this juncture, and took his leave.

As he took his seat in the car beside Walker, Vincent said: "I think that an interview with that bank manager might be useful. It struck me that the hesitation of the lady's manner showed that her connection with Pitt was closer than that which subsists between a lady and her bank cashier. Also she and her chauffeur both lied about her visits to Alice Dodds. We mustn't forget that she is Laurillard's daughter."

"And I suppose it's her brother Charles who runs that drug factory in Belfort," said Walker. "Things seem to be fitting in, don't they? You'll go to the bank manager's private address, I suppose. The bank closed hours ago."

"Yes, we may have to drag him from his dinner table, but I'm sure he'll give us all the help he can."

As soon as Vincent sent in his card, the maid returned to show him into the morning room. Close upon her heels came the bank manager with his table napkin still in his hand.

"I'm sorry to trouble you at this hour," said Vincent, "but I won't keep you more than a minute."

"It's about the Pitt case again, I suppose," said the manager.

"It relates to that case. What I want is any information you can give me about one of your customers, a French lady by birth—a Mrs Pearson."

The manager pondered a moment. "Mrs Pearson? A French lady? I can't tell you very much beyond the fact that she has never overdrawn her account and that she gives us very little trouble."

"Can you tell me whether the late Mr Pitt transacted any business for her outside the ordinary banking business?"

"I can't answer that question offhand, but I can see some of the junior clerks and let you know what they say."

"It might be very helpful if you did. Perhaps you would send me a note addressed to Scotland Yard."

"I will with pleasure. You will, of course, keep my name out of the business?"

"Most certainly."

As they left the bank-manager's house, Vincent said: "I think we've done enough for today. We haven't discovered much, but we have opened up fresh lines of enquiry."

Chapter Seventeen

ON THE following morning a letter marked "Personal" was delivered to Vincent by hand. It was from the bank manager, informing him that registered letters from abroad in stiff envelopes used to arrive at the bank addressed to Mrs Pearson, c/o B. Pitt, Esq., Asiatic Bank. The clerk who gave this information could be seen by Chief Inspector Vincent if he cared to come round to the bank.

Vincent lost no time in setting out for Lombard Street. He was shown into the manager's room and the clerk was sent for. He was an intelligent young man with a good memory.

"Now, Mr Carruthers," said the manager, "I want you to answer any questions which Mr Vincent puts to you. You need not regard any of the bank business as confidential in the matter which Mr Vincent has in hand."

The clerk smiled and turned towards Vincent to invite his questions.

"I understand that you saw the letters that used to come addressed to Mrs Pearson, c/o Mr Pitt. Will you describe what they looked like?"

"Well, they were in thick foolscap envelopes and addressed as you say, but they were marked 'Personal' and 'Confidential', so they were delivered to Mr Pitt."

"Do you know how Mr Pitt disposed of them?"

"Only that he took charge of them to deliver personally to the lady."

"Did it strike you that they contained papers only?"

"Well, now you come to mention it, they seemed to me to be rather more solid than papers would be. Mr Pitt gave me to understand that they contained French notes and certainly there was paid into her account, after one of these letters had arrived, a certain sum of French money."

"When Mrs Pearson called at the bank did she ask for Mr Pitt?"

"No sir, never. She cashed cheques over my counter because I deal with customers whose names begin with a 'P.' That was all the business that she did."

Vincent thanked the manager and made his next call at the National Insurance Bank, where Pitt had had an account. Here he had the task of persuading the manager to allow him to inspect Pitt's account.

"You will understand, of course, that your customer is dead and that I am charged with tracing the cause of his death by the police authorities. Otherwise, I should not have ventured to ask you to allow me to inspect a customer's account."

"I quite understand," replied the manager. "You need not be afraid that I shall put any obstacles in your way. I do not wish to be indiscreet, but I confess that it would interest me to know whether the suspicion of foul play attaches to any particular person."

"It is a little early for me to answer that question," replied Vincent, "but the police authorities are not going to shroud the case in mystery. You will see the result of their enquiries in the press as soon as they are complete."

The manager touched an electric bell on his table. The uniformed messenger appeared. To him was handed a slip of paper to be given to the chief cashier and a minute later the messenger returned bearing a huge ledger.

"You will understand, Mr Vincent, that Mr Pitt closed his account here on the day before his death and his passbook was handed to him. Would not his cheque butts give you all the information you require?"

"No doubt they would if we had them, but they have either been destroyed or stolen from his house. There was a mass of burnt paper in the fireplace of his library. In any case it is the credit side of his account as well that we want."

The manager turned over the leaves of the ledger until he came to the name he was looking for and then pushed the book over to Vincent, who ran his eye down the page.

"You will permit me to make notes, I suppose?" he asked the manager.

"Certainly."

Vincent made rapid notes in pencil in his notebook. The manager watched him, hoping that something would be said to satisfy his curiosity, but when Vincent closed his book and rose to take his leave, he told him nothing.

"Have you got all the information you hoped for?"

"I think so, thanks to your kindness."

"If you could give me a hint of what you are specially looking for, I may be able to help you still further," said the manager, feeling that he was being ruthlessly bereft of a sensation.

"Thank you very much, but I need not trespass further on your kindness. I have found all I want."

It seemed to Vincent a case in which a word from his chief constable would be valuable. He went back to the Central Office and found Richardson alone.

"I'm sorry to bother you again, sir, but I'd like to talk over with you the latest developments in the Pitt case. To begin with, I have established a connection between Pitt and a Mrs Pearson, who is the sister of Charles Laurillard, one of the directors of the drug factory that has just been raided at Belfort in France." He related what he had heard about the registered packages that had been received by Pitt at the bank.

"You think that they contained drugs in powder?"

"I think that it is very probable that they did, but there is no proof."

"Of course the profit accruing from the sale of drugs is large, but so far the methods of importing them that you have discovered would not account for large quantities."

"No sir; I think we shall find that other means are being used. The woman Dodds, who might be useful to us if she were in a fit state to be questioned, is still in the hands of the police surgeon, who says that nothing that she told us in her present state would be reliable. According to information obtained from the landlady of the flats where Alice Dodds lives, a lady in a Lanchester car used to call there to see her. We have ascertained that this car belongs to Mrs Pearson, who denies any knowledge of Alice Dodds. According to the story of her present chauffeur—a Frenchman—it was he who called on the woman unknown to his mistress. I don't think the story is true but I haven't been able to disprove it. I have also discovered that the chauffeur of Pitt was formerly in Mrs Pearson's service."

"Can't you question that chauffeur?"

"I saw him yesterday and I can't say that I took to him. He is drinking. At that time I didn't know that he had worked for Mrs Pearson, but now, of course, I shall see him again."

"A chauffeur out of work can't afford to get drunk at the present price of liquor. He must be getting money from somewhere. Don't lose sight of him on any account."

"In the one interview I had with Alice Dodds she talked about a woman she called 'she', apparently a drug addict. This could not have been Mrs Pearson, who, I am quite sure, is not herself given to drug taking, although probably she supplies it to others."

"The illness of the woman Dodds is bad luck for you, because she changed one of the notes drawn from Pitt's account by himself the day before he was murdered. You haven't traced that any further, I suppose?"

"Not yet, and no more notes have come to light." Vincent opened his notebook. "I made notes just now of certain entries in Pitt's account at the National Insurance Bank. A good deal of money has been passing from Pitt to a man named Thelusson. The only other cheques for large sums drawn on that account were to 'self.'"

"Do you know anything about Thelusson?"

"His was one of the names given me by the chauffeur of people that Pitt used to visit."

"I suppose that you will follow this up?"

"Yes sir; that's what I want to consult you about. Shall I make preliminary enquiries about the man, or go to him direct?"

"You would be in a far stronger position for interviewing him if you armed yourself with information about him. In your place I should get all the information that you can about him confidentially, before you see him. But the thing I want to know is who paid in money to Pitt's account. I suppose you made notes about that?"

"He opened the account in the first place by paying in one hundred pounds in treasury notes. Very few cheques had been paid in—I have the particulars here—but quite frequently, sometimes twice a week, sums were paid in notes."

"Large sums?"

"They varied from fifty to a hundred pounds."

"Was the account large when he closed it?"

"Five thousand six hundred pounds."

"How long had he had the account going?"

"About three years."

"Well, you've got your work cut out in making judicious enquiries about the people who paid in cheques, although I suspect it is the sums that were paid in notes that would interest us most. Let me know the result, but first of all I advise you to concentrate on Thelusson."

"Very good, sir, I will."

Vincent sought out Walker and gave him the list of persons whom he was to question discreetly about cheques paid by them to Pitt.

"I have struck out one of them—Mr Brooklyn— because it will give me an excuse for seeing that gentleman again and getting some further information from him."

"Very good, sir; it shall be done."

Vincent looked at his watch. There was still time for his visit to Brooklyn before lunch. He made his way to Jermyn Street.

Mr Brooklyn, he learned, was at home, but was shortly going out to lunch at his club. He sent up his card and was at once admitted to the flat. He found the gentleman in a more serious mood than on the occasion of his last visit. "Come in,

Mr Vincent," he said; "you are always welcome. What can I do for you?"

"I have come to bother you again about that Pitt case, Mr Brooklyn. I see that a good deal of money seems to have passed from Pitt to a Mr Thelusson. Was this in settlement of gambling debts, do you think?"

Brooklyn wrinkled his brow in thought. "It can scarcely have been that," he said. "Pitt was a careful sort of bloke and no gambler. There was some funny business going on between those two men which I have never been able to make out."

"What was Thelusson's profession?"

"I had always understood that he dealt in fancy soaps and women's beauty apparatus—cosmetics and such like."

"But the sums that passed would have been sufficient to keep the beauty parlours of all London in cosmetics for years. The address which I have for Thelusson is 41, Arkley Street. Do you know if he has his beauty parlour there?"

"Oh no. That is his private flat; I've been there to play cards."

"Does he play for high stakes?"

"He did, sometimes—like the rest of us. If that's a crime I shall plead guilty and take the consequences."

"Did you ever hear a quarrel or a disagreement at any time between Thelusson and Pitt?"

"They had a minor row on one occasion. I fancy Thelusson had reproached Pitt about the kind of friends he entertained and called them 'a b—— lot of thieves'!"

"Was this at Pitt's house or at Thelusson's flat?"

"At Pitt's house in Hampstead."

"Was it the kind of row that might have led to something more serious—you can tell me confidentially."

"No. If you mean was it enough to culminate in murder, the suggestion would be absurd. Thelusson is rather a gay dog. He has plenty of money and he takes life easily; but why don't you call and size him up yourself?"

"I mean to when the proper time comes, but I mustn't take up any more of your time and make you late for lunch."

"That's all right. Come and see me again if you think I can be of any use to you. Good-bye."

Mindful of Richardson's instructions to get all possible information about Thelusson before he called upon him, Vincent resolved to have one more interview with Anton. He drove himself to Hampstead.

He found Anton restored to his usual polite calm. Peace had been unbroken since Vincent's last visit; there had been no disturbing telephone calls; the sensational press had ceased to be interested. Vincent went to the point at once.

"Among the visitors to your late employer, do you remember a Mr Thelusson?"

"Oh yes, sir. Mr Thelusson was a very good friend of Mr Pitt; he came often."

"And they never had a quarrel?"

"Mr Thelusson never quarrelled with Mr Pitt. No, but there were quarrels."

"Who quarrelled?"

"Well, sir, there were loud voices between Mr Blake and Mr Thelusson one night. You could not help hearing," he added apologetically, as if to excuse himself for eavesdropping.

"Of course, I understand that you couldn't help hearing the quarrel. Now think carefully and tell me what you did hear."

"Well, Mr Thelusson, he say Mr Blake is a cheat."

"He meant that he cheated at cards?"

"I suppose so, but they did not mention cards. Mr Thelusson say: 'I have paid you twice, you cheat,' and Mr Blake say: 'You never paid me for last time. You are a worse kind of cheat, a miserly cheat.' They say other words, very bad words."

"Was this long ago?"

"Oh no. Only just before my master went away."

"Did you hear quarrels between Mr Pitt and anyone else?"

"No, Mr Pitt never quarrel. There were never quarrels in this house except that one; that is why I remember it."

"Well, Anton, I'm glad you have a good memory. By the way, has the chauffeur been to see you since?"

"No, he hasn't been again."

"You and the rest of the staff didn't like him?"

"No sir; no one liked him."

"Did Mr Pitt like him?"

"Mr Pitt must have liked him very much, because he let him do what he liked."

"Thank you, Anton. If I think of anything else that you can tell me I will come round here again, and if anything unexpected happens you ring me up immediately."

After a light lunch in the mess-room, Vincent went downstairs and looked into the sergeants' room. He narrowly escaped collision with Walker in the door-way.

"I was just going out again, Mr Vincent. I looked in to see if you had left a message for me."

"I want you to come down to Newquay with me. As you know, the local bench remanded those two rascals in custody and I want to interview them again about some further evidence that has come to hand. They are to come up again tomorrow and unless something fresh transpires we shall have to ask for another remand, so we must get down to Newquay tonight. I suppose you've found nothing compromising about those payments?"

"Only in one case, Mr Vincent, but it's an important one. Among the payments was a cheque drawn by a Miss Hellier for seventy-six pounds. This woman has been up before the Court quite recently on a drug charge and she was reported to the Bench as being a drug addict. The magistrates put her on probation and she is under the care of friends."

"Where can we find her? I should like to have an interview with her before we go down to Newquay."

"I have her address here. Her friends are very well to do. You see, their house is only twenty miles from Charing Cross."

"Have you had your lunch? Yes? Then come along; we'll start at once."

The house proved to be an old Georgian one. They were shown into a library and a few moments later a very charming elderly lady came in, holding Vincent's card in her hand.

"I suppose that you've come to see Miss Hellier. Unless it's absolutely necessary, I would rather give you the information you require myself. This is her hour for resting and we must if possible keep any disturbing influence away from her."

"I'm afraid you may not be able to give me the information I want. It concerns the payment by her of a cheque to the late Mr Bernard Pitt, and I want to know what this payment was for."

She smiled sadly. "I suppose you suspect that it was a payment for drugs."

"Well, to be quite frank, we do."

"Is that the man who was murdered recently?"

"Yes."

"Well, I can tell you that she was greatly upset when she read of the death in the newspapers. In fact she took to her bed for a couple of days."

Vincent saw that she was ready to help him if she could. "I don't want to upset your establishment in any way. The fact is that I have to trace this connection between Miss Hellier and Mr Pitt, and if I am able to do it indirectly through you it will be quite sufficient."

"I will tell you frankly what I have learned from her during the past fortnight. I must tell you that she is the daughter of a very old friend of ours and that she was left a considerable income at his death. She was headstrong and insisted upon living her own life without advice from anyone. I can't tell you when or how she first came to take drugs, but I do know that a few months ago she took into her employment a maid who was herself a drug taker."

"A woman named Alice Dodds?"

"Exactly. You seem to know a great deal about the case."

"As a matter of fact this woman, Alice Dodds, is now detained by the police and is seriously ill in hospital. I wanted to trace the connection between Dodds and a lady who is French by birth and British by marriage."

"I can help you there, I think. The woman was recommended to Miss Hellier by a Mrs Pearson. I must add that the woman Dodds seemed able to obtain as much of the drug as she wanted."

"Thanks to the information you have given me, I need not see Miss Hellier today. I hope that under your care she will continue to improve."

"Thank you, and for my part I am grateful for the help and forbearance shown to us by the police."

Chapter Eighteen

As soon as they were in the car Walker spoke. "So Mrs Pearson was lying when she said that she had no knowledge of Alice Dodds."

"She was, but the important feature is that she should think it worth while to lie over such a trivial matter; she must have had a strong reason: she may have been afraid that Dodds would give her away as a purveyor of drugs."

"I should think that's a strong enough reason. You don't think that it had something to do with that ten pound note that Dodds changed at the bank?"

"I don't think that Mrs Pearson murdered and robbed Pitt if that's what you mean. Pitt withdrew that money from the bank on Friday and was murdered on the following day; he had time to dispose of some money in those twenty-four hours before his death. There's one fact that I don't want to lose sight of, and that is that the chauffeur Arthur Green and Alice Dodds were in Mrs Pearson's service at the same time."

"Don't you think that the chauffeur might have some useful information he could give?"

"I do, but for the present he won't, and Alice Dodds can't tell what they know. Now, with these two men we are going to see at Newquay it may be different. Men of that type are very apt to squeal if they think they can save their own skin by giving their pals away. They've told us this incredible story about the bandit who murdered Pitt and they know it's up to them to help us to prove their story. If there was anyone who had the motive of revenge or robbery for killing Pitt, they must have some idea of his identity. I'm going to question them about Thelusson, although Mr Brooklyn scouted the idea of Thelusson being the murderer."

"I suppose you've never formed a theory that it was Mr Brooklyn himself? When you get one of these cases mixed up with drugs and jealousies and losses at cards, nothing would surprise one."

Vincent laughed. "I got beyond any theory of that kind by finding that Mr Brooklyn had a watertight alibi for that Saturday morning."

As they were approaching Newquay Vincent remarked: "We cannot see any of the prisoners tonight; that must wait until tomorrow morning, but we can have a talk with the police inspector, who may have something useful to tell us."

The car drew up at the police station. The station sergeant relieved them by saying that the inspector would be found upstairs; if they would take the trouble to go up to the first door on the left, he would announce their arrival on his house telephone.

There was an air of relief about the inspector when he shook hands with them. "I fear," he said, "that you can't see any of the prisoners tonight; they will be brought in under escort tomorrow morning in ample time for their appearance in the Court, but it may interest you to know that the two women assert that they are not legally married to the men, and each woman is demanding to be represented by her Consul—in the one case the Austrian and in the other the Russian Consul. Whether these gentlemen will instruct solicitors to represent them at the hearing tomorrow I do not know."

"How did they communicate with their Consuls?"

"The governor of the prison allowed them the use of his telephone for the purpose this afternoon. He rang me up to tell me."

Vincent smiled. "I suppose they are counting upon being tried in this country. If they thought that their trial would take place in France they would begin running round in circles."

"I understand that their defence will be that they knew nothing whatever about drugs being concealed in the hat trimmings; that they bought the hats in good faith from a milliner whose name they gave and they demand that she be sent for."

"They are quite intelligent enough to know that it is very unlikely that this milliner would come and that we can't force her to come. What they don't seem to have realized is that with the aid of a Paris police official whom I know, they could be taken over to France to be tried there and I fancy that it would not be a pleasing prospect for them. The fact is that the French authorities are more in earnest about the drug traffic than we are in England. They have just run to ground a chemical factory where heroin was being made, and closed it. These women were concerned in distributing the poison; they will get no mercy from a French tribunal. Look here, Inspector, can your telephone officer get on to M. Goron" (he spelt the name) "at the Ministry of the Interior, Paris, tomorrow morning at nine? I'll be here to take the call."

"Certainly, I'll warn him at once. The same man will be on duty at nine."

"Good! Then I can get my telephoning over before the prisoners arrive here."

There was nothing more to be done that night. Vincent and Walker went off to their hotel carrying their suitcases.

At nine the next morning Vincent found himself standing over the telephone operator who was ringing up Paris. There was the usual delay, but at last the answer came in the strangulated accent of a far-off French voice trying to pronounce English.

When Vincent was satisfied that he heard Goron at the other end of the wire, he explained briefly the kind of defence that the women were relying upon: "They are throwing the entire blame on to that milliner in the rue Duphot; of course they know that she will not come over to give evidence against them."

"Have no fear, my friend. I want those two women here, and with your permission I will come over and fetch them. I have also other fish to fry—is that not what you say? M. Laurillard, the deputy of whom you know, is taking a holiday in

England at the house of his daughter, we believe. You have her address. It is a holiday demanded by his state of health, since at this moment the air of France would not be conducive to the recovery of his peace of mind."

Vincent laughed. "You have a very neat way of putting these things, my friend."

"So you see, I have two missions to perform in England. First to question M. Laurillard, who has taken himself off to avoid me, secondly to bring back with me those two women. I shall bring with me a female officer of the Sûreté to escort them."

"But will they go with you?" asked Vincent. "Drug trafficking is not an extraditable offence."

"Quite true, but theft is. They stole billheads from Madame Germaine, who is prepared to swear if necessary that they have stolen hats from her also. Have no fear, if they will not come willingly, then I shall bring with me extradition warrants."

"Well, you know your own business best. In this country I should not dare to go so far, but our courts never question an extradition warrant. When will you arrive in England?"

"This afternoon I shall leave by air."

"Then I may be back in time to meet you at Croydon Aerodrome."

The thought of meeting his old friend Goron was a great solace to Vincent, who had been inclined to gird at the legal circumlocution prevalent in his own country as compared with France, where the liberty of the subject was in many directions less consulted than in England. He told the inspector the result of his telephone conversation.

"In that case," said the inspector, "if the women will not go voluntarily I will get the magistrates to back the extradition warrant and we shall be rid of these two creatures, which will be a great relief to everybody concerned. When do you count upon being able to hand me the warrants?"

"Early tomorrow morning, before the Court sits, I hope."

"Very good, Mr Vincent; I'll get the magistrates to remand the women until tomorrow. Will you want to see them before they appear?"

"No, not the women; only the men. I suppose that they have not expressed a wish to make statements since I last saw them."

"Nothing fresh, but both men wrote out statements in prison, which the governor has forwarded to me, containing the story they told you."

"Well, I'd like to see Lewis first. Of the two I think that he is the more likely to squeal."

Vincent had barely time to dictate to Walker notes of his telephone conversation, when the arrival of the prisoners was announced. Lewis was brought into the room by the station sergeant.

"Sit down," said Vincent, who knew the value of having a man's eyes on the level with his own when questioning him. "You made a statement the other day to account for the murder of Mr Pitt. On the face of it your statement was difficult to believe and it is now up to you to modify it or strengthen it by giving additional particulars. Did you know Mr Pitt well?"

"I guess I knew him as well as the other people who played cards with him did."

"When and how did you first meet him?"

"That's quite simple. My friend and I engaged rooms in lodgings in Bloomsbury and he had rooms in the same house. We used to pass each other on the stairs and pass the time of day as you say in this country."

"How long ago was that?"

"Getting on for two years ago."

"When did you first become mixed up with him in selling drugs?"

"I've told you before that I've never been mixed up in the drug traffic."

Vincent held up his hand. "I'd better tell you at once, Mr Lewis, that the French police have just raided the factory in Belfort from which you obtained your stock in trade, so lying about it will not help you. We know more than you think. Let me remind you that in this country the punishment for murder is death, while the punishment for traffic in drugs may be as low as imprisonment for a month with deportation at the end of it. You can only help yourself out of a charge of murder by telling me the plain, unvarnished truth."

"Well, I guess you have me cornered, so get on with your questions and I'll answer them."

"I have already asked you how long ago it was that you got mixed up with Mr Pitt in selling drugs."

"Well, I'll tell you, and you can believe me or not, as you like. We lodged in the same house and one night I and my friend needed a corkscrew. I set out to borrow one from Pitt. I tapped at his door and pushed it a little way open, and there he was sitting at his table with a heap of accounts before him and a camel's hair brush in his hand. There was a little cardboard box with two bottles in it. I knew the stuff. It takes out ink without leaving a trace. He turned green and swept a newspaper on to the table to hide everything and asked me what I wanted in no very polite manner. He said he hadn't got a corkscrew and got rid of me quick. I consulted my friend, who said that he'd been told that the man was cashier in a big bank, so we thought it our duty to tell him where he got off. It wasn't what you would call a pleasant interview with smiles and handshakes, because we put it to him straight that he was robbing his employers and altering the books to hide what he was doing. Of course, we took the high line with him—the Sunday-school line—and talked of acquainting his employers. That brought him down with a bump. So we struck a bargain. We told him that we had stuff to dispose of and if he found us customers for it, which was easy for a man in his position, we'd say nothing about what we'd seen, otherwise we'd feel it our duty to put his directors wise."

"How did you think that a bank cashier could find customers for drugs?"

"We had a better plan than that when we found that the guy thought of nothing but making money. We got him to take that big house in Hampstead."

"Did you pay the rent?" asked Vincent.

"No fear. The guy had made thousands already out of the bank and we persuaded him that he could make thousands more. When we got the house in Hampstead going we introduced one or two people to him and they introduced others, and what with his card parties and peddling the dope and his winnings out of suckers at the card tables, he was a warm man."

"Why did he decide to run away?"

"He got the wind up, because the bank was getting nosey."

"And so you offered to provide him with a passage to France in a motorboat."

"Of course, we couldn't desert a pal when he was in trouble."

"Well, that's clear as far as it goes, but you introduced a number of people to him and they introduced friends of their own. You knew them all and I put it to you that you would know if someone owed him a grudge, sufficiently strong to induce him to commit murder."

"Well, I don't know that, and you may feel sure that if I did I'd have told you before to bear out our statement."

"You guessed that he would be taking a big sum of money with him when he resolved to bolt."

"Why, certainly."

"Did anyone else know that he was leaving the country?"

He hesitated a moment. "Certainly there was one person, but it was a lady."

"You mean Mrs Pearson," said Vincent quietly. "You guys from Scotland Yard seem to know everything. That lady was giving him letters of introduction to her friends in France."

"You mean her father, M. Laurillard."

"I do."

"She used to receive the dope from her father in stout envelopes by registered post addressed c/o Mr Pitt."

"She did. But that doesn't give her a motive for having Pitt done in. He was more use to her alive than dead."

"Was she the only person besides yourselves who knew that he was leaving the country?"

"Well, he had one friend who might have known it."

"You mean Thelusson?"

"Why should you think of him?"

"Pitt was paying large sums of money to him."

"But they had no quarrel."

"I suppose Thelusson is mixed up in this drug business."

"Up to the neck."

"Did Thelusson know that Pitt would be taking a large sum of money away with him?"

"He was likely to make a pretty good guess."

"Well, my sergeant has taken down your answers to my questions and that is all I have to ask you for the present."

The second man, Blake, proved to be less amenable to questioning, but the answers he did give corroborated his companion's statement in every particular. Vincent questioned him further about Thelusson. "You were not always friendly with him?"

"We had words once or twice."

"About payment for dope?"

"Why, yes. He was rolling in money and as mean a louse as crawls on this earth."

"Your quarrel didn't lead to blows?"

"No, only to mudslinging. That guy had no stomach for fisticuffs."

"I have another question to ask you. What do you know about a woman named Alice Dodds?"

"Oh, that woman. She was just running errands for someone else."

"You used to supply her with heroin. You wouldn't have supplied it unless you thought that you were safe in doing so. Who guaranteed her to you?"

"Well, as you seem to know such a lot, I don't mind telling you. It was Laurillard's daughter, Mrs Pearson."

"I thought as much. Mrs Pearson used to employ the woman as her maid. She also employed at one time Arthur Green, Pitt's chauffeur. Was Green ever used by you or Pitt in distributing dope?"

"Not to my knowledge. He wasn't the kind of man that any of us would care to trust."

"Do you think Pitt would have employed him without your knowledge?"

"I guess we should have known it if he had."

"Well, my sergeant has taken down your answers and I've no more questions to put before you appear in Court."

As soon as they were alone Vincent said to Walker: "You and I have seen some crooks in our time, but this little gang would be hard to beat. I want specimens of their handwriting. See whether the inspector will hand over their statements to you, otherwise we must get them photographed. I want to compare them with that anonymous letter received by the bank."

"But wouldn't they have been fools to send such a letter?"

"Not if they made a plan to induce Pitt to bolt. They guessed that he would take a big sum with him and they made their offer of a safe passage out of the country, hoping to rob him on the way."

"Then you think that it was they who committed the murder?"

"No. I think that they planned it, but I'm not sure that their story about a bandit is altogether untrue."

Chapter Nineteen

VINCENT WAS FORTUNATE enough to reach Croydon in time to receive the afternoon airplane from Le Bourget. The great plane circled above the hangars and came to rest exactly on the spot which her pilot was aiming for. The passengers descended the ladder and were shepherded into the shed where landing permits and passports are inspected, but Vincent had been permitted to approach the plane to receive his friend Goron. They shook hands warmly and strolled together towards the barrier. Vincent's car was standing outside.

"I'm glad you've come," said Vincent. "I don't know what powers you've brought with you to compel these women to go with you to France."

"That's all right," said Goron, tapping his breast pocket. "In case they should dig in their toes and refuse to come with me, I have a couple of extradition warrants to shake in their faces. Women, as you know, can be obstinate devils, but a piece of blue paper shoved under their noses is apt to put the fear of God into them. Madame Germaine is in a vindictive mood. She alleges that these women had promised her protection and yet she was taken off and immured at La Roche. The women have not paid for the last hats they ordered from her and she alleges that they stole a handful of her bill-heads from the shop. It was on this that she obtained the extradition warrants."

"I see," said Vincent dryly. "You can do things in France that would be difficult for us in England. But tell me about a much more influential person—M. Laurillard, the deputy."

"Ah! There you have touched upon a thorny subject. In fact you have stamped upon a hornet's nest. From that small beginning of yours in the hat shop of the rue Duphot, you have dragged in another European country, Belgium. That factory at Belfort was supplying many kilogrammes of dope to the Belgian pedlars, always, of course, with the connivance of railway officials. I believe that if we were to make a simultaneous arrest of all men concerned, the trains would cease to run between Paris and Brussels."

"Have you an extradition warrant for Laurillard?"

"Alas! No. As a member of the Chamber he could claim immunity, and so I did not apply for one. Besides, every other deputy in the Chamber would be up in arms to defend him, not knowing, of course, what we might have up our sleeves as regards their own antecedents. What I want to get from Laurillard now is the identity of some of his collaborators on the railway. He is certain to have made some enemies in the railway service, men who thought that he ought to have paid them more than he did and he will not be above denouncing them."

"Well, I am driving you straight to Madame Pearson's house for this momentous interview, and I myself will accompany you as I have questions to put to the lady. Have you brought any female escort with you?"

"She is crossing by boat and will find her own way by rail to Newquay."

For the rest of the drive Vincent tried to satisfy Goron's appetite for information about his own work in the hunting of Pitt's murderer since they last met.

"You think that this wild story about a bandit on an English high road can be true?"

"I do, but I have a big task before me in getting proof of my theory. But here we are. This is the street where Mrs Pearson lives."

The maidservant who opened the door appeared surprised when they asked for Monsieur Laurillard. "Yes," she said; "he is here, but he only arrived this morning and he's been resting in his room ever since."

"This gentleman has come all the way from Paris to see him. We will wait inside while you explain this to your mistress. Here is my card."

She showed them into the dining room and ten minutes later the door opened to admit Mrs Pearson. They rose as she came in.

"My father is resting," she said, "and I cannot disturb him now."

"You might take me to his bedside, madame," said Goron, diplomatically. "A few minutes of conversation is all that I require."

"He's not in bed; he is resting in an armchair. He may even be asleep, but as you insist even after I have told you this I must take you up to his room."

"And perhaps when you have introduced this gentleman to your father's room, you will return here. I have one or two questions to ask you," said Vincent.

"Are you still concerned about that former chauffeur of mine—Arthur Green?"

"Yes, and about one or two other matters in which you can enlighten me."

There was no undue delay about her return to the dining room. She entered holding her head high, hoping perhaps to induce in her visitor a sense of shame at intruding on her privacy. She made no motion towards a chair and the interview took place standing, she retaining the door handle in her hand.

These were not the conditions under which friendly meetings are conducted, but Vincent felt himself quite equal to measuring weapons with her.

"When we last met, Mrs Pearson, I asked you a question about a woman named Alice Dodds and you told me that you had never employed a woman of that name. May I ask why you thought it proper to tell me an untruth? You must have had some reason, because a lady in your position would naturally tell the truth in answer to a direct question."

She hesitated scarcely an instant before making her reply. "If I misled you it was in the interest of the woman herself. I did not care to take away her character and so—naturally..."

"And so, naturally, you told me an untruth?"

"If you like to put it that way, I have no objection."

"You feel, no doubt, that there is no harm in deceiving a police officer, in fact that it can be a meritorious act to do so. I suppose this explains why you told me another untruth."

"Indeed?" said the lady with the sweetest smile. "You told me that your only knowledge of Mr Pitt was just the slight acquaintance which a customer has of a bank official when they stand with the counter between them."

"Did I?" smiled the lady.

"You forgot to mention those registered packages that Mr Pitt used to receive for you."

"Registered packages?"

"Yes. Packages containing heroin." Vincent was determined to drag the lady from the saddle of her high horse, but it was not a very easy manoeuvre.

"Mr Pitt is dead. You are trying to fabricate dramatic evidence. I don't know why."

"The evidence I have is not fabricated, I assure you, madame. If you ever have to meet it in court I fear that your counsel will have his work cut out for him."

"You are trying to frighten me."

"I must have the truth and you will do yourself no good by giving me false answers. You keep a wages book, I suppose. I want to know from your wages book the exact dates when Arthur Green and Alice Dodds were in your service. In fact, I should like to see your wages book for myself."

She shrugged her shoulders. "If you will wait here I will go and get the book."

When the book was brought and opened at the appropriate page she said: "It is lucky that I did not destroy this book as so many people do. You will see that it relates to last year, not this one."

Vincent studied the pages, making notes in his pocketbook. "I see from this book," he said, "that these two people were in your service at one and the same time. That is what I wanted to know." He shut the book and handed it back to her.

"One more question before I go. Did Mr Pitt ever pay you for goods with which you supplied him?" Her surprise at this question was so genuine that Vincent could not think that she was lying when she said: "Never."

"Did you ever ring up the late Mr Pitt's house in Hampstead?"

"Never."

"Not even after his death, when you thought that Mr Blake and Mr Lewis might be hiding there?"

"Never."

"Did Arthur Green, the chauffeur, ever act as messenger between you and Mr Pitt?"

"Certainly not. When Arthur Green left my employment I had nothing more to do with him."

"Thank you, Mrs Pearson," said Vincent, taking up his hat. "You will, perhaps, permit me to wait here until my friend has finished his business with your father."

"Certainly," she replied coldly before she withdrew. Five minutes later Goron joined him with an air of elation. "I made him talk," he said, "and he gave me everything I needed."

"Names?"

"Oh yes; he'd no scruples about giving away his friends. There may be honour among thieves, but honour does not rank high among drug traffickers."

"Well, as we both have gained our points, we are free to leave the house."

At the door Vincent drew the uniformed porter aside and asked him: "Do you know where Mrs Pearson garages her car?"

"Yes sir; it's that Plimsoll's garage round the corner."

As they walked to their own car which had been parked a few doors away, Vincent explained to Goron that he wished to interview the French chauffeur of Mrs Pearson and suggested that they should go together to the garage. They were lucky enough to find the chauffeur at work on the car.

"It might be useful if you asked him in French what has gone wrong with the car. He will be startled by being addressed suddenly in his own language."

Goron took the hint. The man looked up startled and faced his questioners, then when he recognized Vincent he became agitated and threw down his tools on the concrete floor. Goron took advantage of his state of alarm by saying sternly in French: "You will answer all the questions put to you by this gentleman and answer them truthfully or it may go hardly with you."

In reply to Vincent's questions they drew from him the admission that he had lied about Alice Dodds. He himself had never seen the woman. He drove his mistress of the house and was paid by her to keep his mouth shut about it. If he was ever questioned he was to tell the lie that he had told Vincent. They were satisfied that they had extracted all the material truth from him and they returned to their car.

"Now," said Goron, "I must ask you to find me a hotel, for I don't propose to go down to Newquay until tomorrow morning."

"You will come with me to my lodging; my landlady will give you a bedroom and it will delight the poor soul to be allowed to provide us with a meal; she is no mean cook. If you don't mind making a little detour in the car, I want to catch my sergeant and then we shall be free."

Goron was far too much interested in watching the control of the London traffic to do anything but approve, and they drove through the iron gate which leads into New Scotland Yard. Goron was left in the car while Vincent disappeared into the postern door of police headquarters. He dug Walker out of the sergeants' room and gave him his instructions in the passage.

"I want that fellow Green watched. You understand that the observation must be very discreet. Those little houses up in north London are difficult to keep under discreet observation, but if any man can do it you can."

"Have you any fresh evidence?"

"Not much, but I've reason to believe that there's some connection between him and the woman Dodds. They were in service together with Mrs Pearson and if you remember Anton told us that the chauffeur called one morning and asked whether a lady had rung up. It happened that Alice Dodds had rung up on the previous evening."

"You want me to do this job myself."

"Yes, because the man must on no account be scared off. I have not yet seen Thelusson but shall interview him tomorrow."

"Then you have formed a theory about that chauffeur."

Vincent nodded. "Early tomorrow morning I want you to dig out the statements of the servants in Hampstead that you took down on our first visit to the house."

Vincent devoted the rest of the evening to entertaining his friend Goron, whose visits to London had been rare. At breakfast on the following morning Goron remarked: "If I'm going down to Newquay today I shall need an interpreter."

"Certainly. I've arranged for that already. You will take one of our French-speaking officers, Sergeant Campion, with you. He has been warned to be ready."

Having seen Goron safely off to Newquay with his detective interpreter, Vincent decided that it would not be too soon to call upon the tenant of 41, Arkley Street. The door of the flat was opened by a manservant who exuded discretion from every pore. From him Vincent learned that his employer was at home and he was shown into a sumptuously furnished room. Like all detective officers, Vincent was quick to appraise the financial status of the man he had come to see. The flat was roomy and well- but not over-furnished, in the labour-saving modern style in which there is nothing to catch dust. Its owner bustled in holding Vincent's card in his hand.

He was a man not much over thirty, rather thickset and he looked overfed—certainly, in Vincent's opinion, not the type of man who would hold up a car in the road and act as a bandit. Vincent plunged into business at once.

"You knew the late Mr Bernard Pitt."

The man hesitated a second before replying: "I did."

"You had certain monetary transactions with him."

"We played cards together sometimes."

"Did Mr Pitt lose heavily to you?"

"No, sometimes he won and sometimes he lost a bit, as always happens with cards."

"But the money transactions that I'm thinking of were for large sums and always from Mr Pitt to you."

"That's quite possible. We transacted business together. I sold him goods and he always settled on the nail."

"What kind of goods?"

"Fancy soap, principally. I import this soap from France and retailed it to Pitt and others."

"Can you tell me what Mr Pitt did with the large quantity of soap you supplied to him?"

"I always understood that he retailed it to other people."

"I suppose you've no objection to my looking through your books?"

"Not at all, but they are not here. You would have to come to my place of business."

"It must be nearly time for you to be starting. Couldn't we go together?"

"If you like." The tone was not cordial, but Vincent thought it better to appear as if he were accepting an invitation. Thelusson refused a lift in Vincent's car on the ground that his own was waiting for him.

"Then," said Vincent blandly, "perhaps you'll give me a lift in your car and I'll leave mine in the car park here and come back for it." He was not going to allow Thelusson to escape from his sight.

The car set them down at the beauty parlour, which was as sumptuously furnished as its owner's flat. Evidently business was in full swing; every little room was occupied by ladies who were in the hands of hairdressers, manicurists and the like. It didn't take Vincent long to decide that if Thelusson were engaged in the drug traffic it was a side line which had nothing to do with his customers.

Thelusson conducted him into the office and laid a pile of books before him with an air of polite boredom.

Before opening any of the books Vincent asked: "Where is your store-room?"

Thelusson pointed to a door leading out of the office. Vincent opened the day book and ran through the names; there was nothing suspicious about the entries in this book or in the others that he examined. There were names of well-known hairdressers with invoices of goods, but the name of Pitt was not among them.

"Where did you keep Mr Pitt's account?" asked Vincent.

"I destroyed his invoices when he died to avoid the risk of my clerk sending an account to a dead man."

Vincent turned over the pages of the ledger. "I don't see that any pages have been taken out of this book. Did you keep a special ledger for Mr Pitt?"

"I did. He was my most important customer."

Vincent made notes of the names and addresses of the firms who had been supplied with soap and other requisites. Thelusson watched him contemptuously, as who should say, "this is how public money is wasted." But when Vincent turned to him for permission to enter the storeroom he observed that the expression changed to one of concern. The permission was given, however, and Vincent found himself in the presence of dozens of boxes of soap. There were a few packing cases nailed down and addressed ready to be delivered. One case was not addressed nor was it fully filled. Vincent dived his hand into it and took out a cake of soap.

"I'll take this away if you don't mind," he said, as he put it into his pocket. Thelusson gave an inarticulate grunt. It was clear from his expression that he minded very much indeed.

Vincent hailed a taxi and drove to the park where he had left his car; thence he made a beeline for police headquarters and ran up the stone staircase that led to the laboratory. He explained to the white-coated officer in charge what he wanted. The man shook the cake of soap close to his ear.

"It seems all right in weight, Mr Vincent," he said. "What do you think is wrong with it?"

"I can't say until you have got to work on it with your dissecting knife or whatever surgical instrument you use."

The laboratory assistant smiled. "That's soon done, Mr Vincent." He took the soap to a table which he covered with white paper and used a boring tool. At first flakes of soap were detached, but presently the tool encountered something less solid. A few grains of white powder escaped from the orifice and were lost among the soap flakes.

"Why, the cake's hollow!" exclaimed the assistant. "You didn't warn me of that."

"I did not, because I didn't know it until you made that hole in it."

Chapter Twenty

ON HIS WAY down from the laboratory a detective patrol stopped Vincent as he was stepping out of the lift.

"Sergeant Walker has been looking for you and instructed me to let him know as soon as I found you. I think he has something important to tell you."

"Very good. Tell him to come to my room."

A few minutes later there was a tap on the door and Walker came in, shutting the door carefully behind him.

"You've something fresh to tell me?"

"Yes sir. When I got out to Palmer's Green last night I found a notice 'To Let' on the gate of Green's house. The next-door people told me that the Greens left the day before and they did not know where they had gone. So I dropped into the local pub and got into conversation with the barman over my beer. He was a forthcoming kind of man. He said that he knew Arthur Green well. 'Often in here?' I asked. 'That's right; he's been one of my best customers. If he carries on the same way in the place he's gone to, all his profits will go down his throat. I never knew such a chap for putting it away.' 'Got his own place now, has he?' I asked. 'Yes, a motor garage down at Alton, in Hampshire. He bought it from me and paid a good price for it.' I asked him whether he'd paid for it in cash. 'Lor' bless you, no. He paid for it with a cheque.' 'Oh, then Arthur Green has gone up in the world—runs to a banking account of his own,' I said. 'No, the cheque was signed by the gentleman who's financing him.' 'An old employer, I suppose,' I said. 'I think so.' 'Was the name Pitt?' I asked. 'Oh no,' he said; 'it was a long name and I can't pronounce it, but I'll spell it for you.' And then he spelt the name of Thelusson," said Walker.

"You did very well in getting all that information out of the barman," said Vincent. "Of course, you got the address of the garage that the man's gone to."

"Oh yes, I've got that all right."

"Well, if he's just taken a garage of his own, he's not likely to give us the slip. I must see Thelusson again and hear his version of how Green came by that cheque."

"Do you want me to go down to Hampshire and look him up?"

"Not yet. Have you dug out those statements of Pitt's servants that we took from them in the beginning?"

"Yes. I have them here."

Vincent read the statements and then gave a satisfied click of his tongue.

"Ah! Perhaps you've noticed the discrepancy between the statements of Anton and the chauffeur as to what happened. The chauffeur said he was given special leave on that Saturday and Anton said that the chauffeur always had Saturdays off. The chauffeur said that Pitt often dined out on Saturdays and Anton said that he always gave a dinner party at home. You know the lie of the land. It would have been quite possible for the chauffeur to take the car out without the other servants' knowledge. While I'm visiting Thelusson I'd like you to slip round to the garage and make a note of the last day's run of the speedometer. Green may have forgotten to change it to zero. There was a heavy thunderstorm that morning; you might see whether the wheels are muddy."

Vincent wondered whether Thelusson had already taken to his heels in consequence of the cake of soap that had been taken from his storeroom, but to his relief he found him sitting in his little office apparently without a care on his mind.

"You import a remarkable kind of soap, Mr Thelusson."

"You think so? It is very much in request on account of its nutritive properties for the hair."

"I can well believe that there is a sale for it, but I haven't come to see you about that now. That will be gone into by the proper authorities. What I have come for is to know how you came to give a cheque for a fairly large sum to the chauffeur of the late Mr Pitt?"

"Well, Pitt was a friend of mine and the chauffeur came to me with a hard-luck story about not being able to get a job and said that a small outlay in capital would put him in possession of a valuable motor garage and so I advanced him the money."

"I see," said Vincent dryly. "It would be quite incorrect for anyone to say that you paid him that as hush money?"

"Hush money? What do you mean?"

"Perhaps my next question will make my meaning clearer. Did you sign or did he sign any agreement for repaying this loan?"

"No. It was a verbal agreement between us that he would repay it at some future time."

"A rather curious way of doing business, wasn't it?"

"Well, of course, I knew the man and that makes all the difference."

"You knew the man and that made all the difference? And you knew of course that a man in that position might talk and so you thought that you would put him under an obligation. Evidently you do not know the ways of blackmailers as well as I do."

"Blackmailers!"

"Yes, that is the word I used, because Green was blackmailing you. He knew something about you that might be very compromising if it came out."

"I don't know what you're talking about."

"Well, let me put it a little more plainly. You know, of course, that Pitt was murdered. The car in which he was travelling was stopped by a man who entered it and shot him through the head. This man may have been someone who wished to get rid of Pitt, or he may have been hired by some-one else."

Thelusson sprang to his feet. "This is outrageous. Do you dare to suggest that I hired Green as an assassin to shoot Pitt?"

"That theory had crossed my mind," said Vincent calm-ly. "Of course, if you can suggest any other reason why he should be blackmailing you, I shall be glad to listen to it."

Thelusson took two turns up and down the room and then stopped opposite Vincent. "I suppose the game's up. You have that cake of soap and you'll have it analyzed, and so I may as well own up."

"I must caution you that I shall take down what you say in writing."

"Never mind that. It's better to come before a court for drug trafficking than for murder. Green was demanding hush money because he knew that I was importing drugs. He had been blackmailing Pitt also."

"Are you sure of that?"

"Quite sure, and Green himself told me that Pitt had promised him two thousand pounds to clear out of the coun-try, but it was Pitt who was trying to clear out without keep-ing his promise."

"Did Green tell you that he knew that Pitt was going to leave the country?"

"I gathered that he knew because he said that instead of helping him to leave the country, Pitt was clearing out abroad himself."

"You are quite sure that he put it in that way?"

"Yes, quite, and he talked a lot about Pitt's meanness as he (Green) was anxious to leave the country and Pitt knew it."

"Did he say why he wished to get out of the country?"

"He told me that there was a woman who had taken to drugs and he wanted to get her abroad to lead a new life.

I don't know if the woman was a relation. I didn't ask him any more details but he blamed Pitt and his associates for her downfall."

Vincent sprang an apparently irrelevant question upon him. "Do you know a Mrs Pearson?"

"I do, and as I'm making a statement I may as well tell you that it is through her agents that I imported that stuff for Pitt. All the other soap and cosmetics that I import are pure. The special soap of which you were able to secure a sample was imported for Pitt. I have no personal customers for it and I don't know who his customers were."

"Wasn't it risky leaving the case open in your storeroom?"

"Not at all. I give out all goods from the storeroom and none of my assistants is allowed to help herself."

"Did Arthur Green mention Mrs Pearson as one of the people who had helped to ruin this woman?"

"As a matter of fact he did."

"Now, Mr Thelusson, you are in the unauthorized possession of dangerous drugs and are liable to prosecution, but if you show yourself ready to help the authorities a prosecution need not necessarily follow. I need not disguise from you that the people we want to get at are Mrs Pearson and her little gang. I shall recommend you to my colleagues as a useful informant. Personally, I am engaged in hunting down the murderer of Pitt. Do you know of anyone in this band of drug traffickers who had a motive for getting rid of Pitt?"

"Frankly, I can't say I do. You know, of course, of the case of Miss Hellier. I believe that Mrs Pearson was badly frightened over that case, thinking that she would be dragged into it as purveyor of the drugs, but I don't think that Pitt's share in the drug traffic was known to many people. He was so clever."

"Well, thank you, Mr Thelusson. That's all that I have to ask you now."

"So I have to sit here wondering when the axe will fall on me. It's not a pleasant position for a businessman to be in."

"I can well understand that, and I'm afraid I can say nothing at this juncture to relieve your anxiety. I must leave you now to get on with other pressing work."

On reaching the Yard, Vincent found that Sergeant Walker had already returned from his visit to the garage in Hampstead.

"Well, what about that speedometer?"

"It's all right; the record of the last run had been left untouched; it would just have accounted for a run to Oldbury and back, but the car had no mud on it except a little on the underside of the wings."

"Of course, he would have cleaned off the mud. Now I've discovered that Pitt had promised that chauffeur two thousand pounds and was leaving the country without paying it. That gives us a motive for the crime."

"But if the chauffeur waylaid Pitt and killed and robbed him, what can he have done with the money, because he got the cheque out of Thelusson to pay for that garage?"

"Oh, I think that he's taking no risks, he's afraid to change any of the notes for fear that they may be traced. Besides establishing a motive for the crime I think I've found a closer connection between Alice Dodds and Green; the only note that has come to light out of the sum which Pitt withdrew from his bank was changed by Alice Dodds. I wish to heaven that woman would get well enough to be questioned."

"Have you seen the doctor's report upon her this morning? It was pretty bad."

"Yes, it was; there's some doubt as to whether she'll recover. I'm wondering if that accounts for the purchase of that garage by Arthur Green."

"You mean that he doesn't intend to bolt out of the country?"

"According to Thelusson's story he had some young woman who had taken to drugs and whom he wanted to rescue by taking her abroad. I think you'd better slip down to Hampshire and find out what you can on the spot. We are going to have difficulty in bringing this crime home if he is the guilty person. There comes a moment in every case when one has to rely upon luck and I think that that moment has come. I feel quite sure that Green knew that his master intended to leave the country on that Saturday morning. You get off to Hampshire as quick as you can. I'm going round again to that garage where Pitt hired the car."

On arriving at the garage in Bloomsbury, Vincent sought out the proprietor.

"Have you got your car back from Newquay yet?" he asked.

"No, not yet, but I know it's safe down there so I'm not worrying."

"You told me when I was here before that after you had let out that car another garagist came in and told you that they had been to him first. What was he like?"

"He was a youngish man, pretty ordinary looking, of about my height but stouter built than I am. He had a very gruff sort of voice and was what I should call a grouser."

"Can you remember what questions he asked you?"

"He asked me very particularly what car I was lending them."

"Did you show it to him?"

"I did and he looked it well over. Then he said: 'Oh well, that's a smarter car than I could have lent them.'"

"Can you remember whether he asked you at what time they wanted to take the car?"

"Yes, he asked me that, and though I didn't see what business it was of his, I told him that they wanted it at eight o'clock. He made some excuse about being so inquisitive and said: 'Oh, I couldn't have got them the kind they wanted in time.' I can't remember any more that he said."

"I may want you to pick him out from a dozen men a little later," said Vincent. "I hope you've got a good memory for faces."

"Pretty good, I fancy."

When Vincent got back to his office table he found cause to remember what he had said to Walker—that there comes a time in every case when one has to rely upon luck. Lying on his table was a note from the telephone room.

"For Chief Inspector Vincent from Inspector Collins of Hampstead. The woman Alice Dodds is now lucid, though still very ill. The doctor certifies that she is fit to reply to questions."

Carrying the message with him, Vincent set out for the hospital.

Chapter Twenty-One

WHEN VINCENT ARRIVED at the Cottage Hospital the police doctor from Hampstead met him in the corridor.

"I must explain why you find me here. The woman Alice Dodds is extremely ill and not likely to recover. Besides being a drug addict she is in an advanced stage of cardiac disease, and knowing that you had important questions to put to her, I thought that I had better be within call. She is now conscious and her mind seems to be clearer than it has been at any time since she was brought here, so now is your moment for putting questions to her."

"You think that she cannot recover?"

"Yes, I doubt whether she will last out the day; she is beyond all medical help. If you will follow me into the ward I'll introduce you to the nursing Sister."

Vincent would have found it difficult to recognize the patient if she had not been pointed out to him.

He shook hands with the Sister, who warned him not to say anything to excite the patient if he could help it.

"She keeps asking for a person named Arthur Green," said the Sister, "but she is unable to indicate where he can be found."

"I can soon find Arthur Green," said Vincent. "Has she said why she is so anxious to see him?"

"She is quite conscious that she is dying and she wants to give him something—some paper I gather that it is."

"It is important that I should be present when she hands over this paper. I suppose that this can be arranged."

The Sister looked round the ward. "I could put you behind that screen so that you could hear what passes between them."

"Very well, then I will ask the matron superintendent to allow me to use her telephone before I see Alice Dodds."

He asked the matron to put through a call to the police station at Alton, and in a very few minutes the connection was made.

"Is that the superintendent at Alton?"

"Who is speaking?"

"Chief Inspector Vincent from Scotland Yard. I want to speak to Sergeant Walker from the Yard if you know where to find him."

"He's in the office at this moment. If you'll hold on I'll call him to the phone."

Vincent felt immensely relieved when he heard the voice he knew. He asked: "Have you located Arthur Green yet?"

"Yes, I have; but I haven't had time to see him yet; I've only just arrived. Luckily the local police knew where to find him."

"I want you to bring him back to London as soon as you can. You can tell him that Alice Dodds is dying in hospital and keeps asking for him. That ought to make him come willingly."

"Very good. I'll get hold of him at once. Where shall I bring him to?"

"To the Cottage Hospital at Hampstead. I shall be there."

"Very good, but I can't be up in Town in much under two hours."

"That will bring us to about seven o'clock. That will do all right. You can be as lavish as you like in taking taxis because every minute counts."

"Very good. I'll start off at once."

Vincent returned to the ward and approached the Sister.

"Is the woman still conscious?"

"Yes."

"Then I can speak to her now."

The Sister surrendered her chair by the bedside to Vincent and took her stand behind him to watch the patient.

Vincent bent over the pillow and asked softly: "You wish to see Arthur Green?"

"Yes," she said faintly.

"I've sent for him. He will be here in an hour or so. You know Arthur Green well?"

"Yes, very well," she murmured with the ghost of a smile.

"In fact he wanted to take you out of the country and make you well."

"But there was his mother; he had to get her settled first."

The Sister looked warningly at Vincent.

"I've only one more question to ask," he said. "Arthur Green gave you a ten-pound note not long ago."

"Yes."

Vincent rose and patted the wasted hand of the patient. "That's all I wanted to ask, Sister."

On leaving the hospital he told the Matron that he would return in time to meet his sergeant and Arthur Green. He had nearly two hours to dispose of—time to go back to the Yard and put through a call to Newquay and exchange news with his friend Goron. It took some little time to put the call through but in the end he learned that Goron was actually in the police office and would be summoned to the telephone.

After the usual greetings that French officials consider essential, Goron came to business.

"I have brought those two women to reason. They will cross to France tomorrow."

"Then shall I not see you again?" asked Vincent. "Oh yes. I shall bring them with their female escort up to London by the nine o'clock train which gets in early tomorrow morning. Then I can spend a short time with you before taking them across; we shall have quite a lot to discuss. How are you getting on with your end of the case?"

"I am on the right trail, I feel sure, but my difficulty is to get proof of what I know to be the truth. I will meet your train tomorrow morning and you will come back to breakfast with me."

Vincent had plenty of occupation in writing up his report of the case while he was waiting. He left again for the hospital in good time.

It was seven o'clock when Walker arrived with his man—more than an hour after the hour when visitors are turned out. As Vincent had expected, Green was in a sullen mood. He had been persuaded to come against his will. By arrangement with the lady superintendent he was taken straight to the bedside of Alice Dodds.

Vincent was already in his place behind the screen. The nurse had told him that Alice Dodds refused to be parted from her handbag. Her voice was so weak that from his listening post he could not catch her words, but he was in a position to see what passed. Her lips moved and Green leaned forward to listen. She handed her bag to him; he opened it and took out from it an envelope which he put in his breast pocket.

After a very short exchange of whispered words between the two the Sister intervened and turned both Green and Vincent out of the ward, arranging screens round the bed.

The two men met in the corridor.

"I want that envelope that Alice Dodds has just given to you," said Vincent firmly.

"I've no doubt you do," was the surly reply. "You police can't even respect the wishes of a dying woman."

"Unless you hand over that envelope it will be my duty to arrest you as an accessory to a felony."

"All very pretty and nice, but you can't scare me with your legal police terms."

"You refuse then to hand over that envelope?"

"I invite you to come and take it."

"Very well, then I arrest you as an accessory to a crime. You'll come quietly to the station, or would you prefer me to call a uniformed constable to help me take you there?"

Vincent could see that the other was measuring his chances of using violence and making his escape after delivering a smashing blow in the face. Prudence prevailed, however. "We don't want a row in a hospital," the man said. "I'll come quietly with you to the station."

Vincent was taking no chances. Walker was at the other end of the corridor and he signed to him to approach.

"Slip down to the telephone and ask the superintendent to send up a couple of reserve patrols to lend us a hand."

The show of force had apparently led Green to drop his intention of resistance or escape, for he fell into a sullen silence and accompanied them to the police station. There he was charged with having been in possession of the stolen banknote which he had given to Alice Dodds.

"You think yourselves very clever," he said; "but Mr Pitt gave me that banknote on the day before he went away."

The reply was taken down and Vincent proceeded to search him. In the envelope taken from his breast pocket he found a safe deposit receipt for a box deposited with Messrs Wrench and Company.

"Keep this man in custody until we return from Wrench and Co.," said Vincent. "We shall bring back the box with us."

Green broke out into noisy protests against what he called interference with his private property, but Vincent replied courteously that provided that all the property in the box proved to be his he had nothing at all to fear.

Walker accompanied Vincent to Wrench's emporium and there, after some delay in convincing the managing director that he must hand over the box in return for an official receipt from the police, they were allowed to take it away. It was a white wood box fortified with iron angle plates.

On arriving back at the police station, Green was asked for the key. He said that he had left it at his home in Hampshire and that in any case the police had no right to open it.

"It will be opened in your presence," said Vincent; "and you can see that everything taken out of it is replaced provided that there is nothing in it to which you have no right. Get a hammer and chisel, Walker."

The tools were brought and at the second blow of the hammer the lock gave way. The box contained nothing but a leather cash bag such as bank messengers use. That, too, had to be opened forcibly, since Green declined to supply a key.

It was packed with Bank of England notes of varying denominations and at the bottom lay a passbook of the National Insurance Bank in the name of Bernard Pitt.

Vincent turned towards Green, from whom all truculence had now disappeared. "Arthur Green, I arrest you for the murder of Bernard Pitt by shooting him through the head. You are not obliged to make any statement."

Goron and Vincent breakfasted together half an hour after the arrival of the train from Newquay.

"So you have arrested the man you believe to be the murderer of Pitt," said Goron; "and that fantastic story told by those Americans is true after all."

"Yes."

"What interests me keenly is the difference between criminal procedure in England and its counterpart in my own country. There is a refreshing finality about your English procedure. With us a lawyer would be briefed; there would be interminable delays; the case would be carried to the Cours de Cassation and thence to I know not what legal authorities until it reached the President of the Republic. By that time the wretched prisoner would have been languishing in jail for perhaps two years. With you there is only one appeal."

"Yes, when the Court of Criminal Appeal has pronounced its decision the matter is ended except for private petitions to the Home Secretary for a respite of the sentence; such respites are very rarely given."

"That is why violent crime is less common in England than it is in France. Your justice is not only sure but swift and that is the secret of judicial administration. But now tell me, confidentially, has your man made a confession?"

"No, we do not press our prisoners to confess, but we do not bring him to justice until the case against him is watertight enough to satisfy the Director of Public Prosecutions."

Goron heaved a sigh. "Ah! If only politics were not in-volved in criminal cases, it might be the same with us. People are apt to say that the democratic institutions of our two countries are the same. Alas! There is a wide difference. No political party would dare to interfere with judicial punishments in England; whereas with us...But tell me, how do you regard your case as watertight?"

"Well, the story that Blake and Lewis told was that their car was held up in the road by a masked bandit who killed Pitt and made off with a bag of money. That money, consisting of notes that could be identified, was found in Green's possession, and, what is more, a search of his room revealed a black mask hidden in a drawer."

"How strange that criminals should so often preserve objects that bring the crime home to them! Was his motive only robbery?"

"Partly revenge, I think. It appears that at one time he was a fellow employee of a woman named Alice Dodds; they were in the service of Mrs Pearson, Laurillard's daughter. She employed Dodds over the drug traffic, with the inevitable result that Dodds herself took to drugs. After that Green took service with Pitt and blackmailed him. Pitt promised to give him two thousand pounds to clear out of the country with his young woman, Dodds, but Green discovered that Pitt was on the point of leaving England himself without redeeming his promise. That, in my opinion, supplied the motive. From enquiries I have made, Green found out the make of car that Pitt was hiring and his time of departure. He lay in wait for him in the open road and shot him."

"And so while you were hunting for the murderer in France he was here under your very nose."

"Had Pitt's companions been just ordinary law-abiding passengers they would have denounced the murderer and he would have been run to ground sooner, but they were criminals with much to hide and Pitt himself was no flower; he was bolting with money stolen from his employers."

"A pretty nest of rascals. But why didn't Arthur Green make his escape while there was time?"

"To do him justice I think he was trying to persuade the woman to go with him and she was in such an advanced state of addiction to drugs that she hung back. Then, apparently, he was afraid to use the money because the numbers of the notes were known."

"It seems to me," said Goron, "that the person who deserves the heaviest punishment is Laurillard's daughter, Mrs Pearson."

"Yes, the sinister part of it is that she will escape scot free."

"Never mind, my friend, in hunting down your murderer, you have rendered a signal service to us in France. You have enabled us to close down another of these poison factories which were sapping the strength of our youth. These young people began poisoning themselves from a sense of adventure, the sense that assails most young people at some time of wishing to defy the law."

"Yes, if the sacrifice of Alice Dodds and of this young fool, Green, could be a warning to others, their deaths will expiate their follies."

THE END

Made in the USA
Middletown, DE
29 November 2018